THE JEWELLED EGG
MURDERS

VIRGINIA WINTERS

From The River Publishing

For my family

Chapter One

Anne slumped against the edge of a crate, a few metres from the young woman's body. A single dark hole pierced the white skin of the forehead above her eyes. Her head had fallen to the left as she died, and a trickle of blood had oozed from the wound, coursed into the left ear and out, and congealed on the dirty grey floor of the loading area where she lay. On the wall behind, a spray of blood and brain traced a pattern. Anne touched the face with the back of her hand. Cold. She sought a pulse in the thin neck but found nothing. She turned away from the clouded blue eyes. She dialled 911 and moved back into the store and sat. So young, she thought. Her hands trembled. What was this? She'd seen the dead before. Not so often in her life, paediatricians didn't, but lately... She wanted to be sure, to touch the young woman again, but she shouldn't. No way to explain why she would do that.

Three bodies in as many years, she thought. Would they be suspicious of her this time? That happened before, in Bermuda. She rubbed her hands on the soft fabric of her pale blue parka and shivered, cold in spite of her warm coat. Silence flowed from the body on the floor and surrounded her, until it was broken by the wail of sirens. Could she face the questions alone? No, not again. She punched in Thomas's number on her cell phone.

"Thomas, I'm at Erin's shop. There's a body"

"Erin?"

"No. The police are coming."

"I'll be right there."

~

Two days before, she sat in the jaunty yellow Beechcraft Bonanza that Thomas used to commute between Toronto, New York and his mother's home in Vermont. The plane was larger and, Anne hoped, safer, than the one they had ploughed into a field on a previous trip to New Hampshire. This time, they were flying in for Christmas with Thomas's family. Below, a single runway, a ploughed line through the snow, rose to meet the plane. A young man with Thomas's dark hair and lithe build stood at the entrance to the Quonset hut that served as a terminal. His red and black ski jacket stood out against the aluminum of the building.

"Daniel's waiting," Thomas said. "I told him we'd take a cab."

Tension in his voice.

"Do you think something's wrong?"

"Perhaps my mother. She sounded vague on the phone the last couple of times I talked to her."

"You didn't say anything—"

"You have enough."

A muscle knotted over the sharply-defined bone of his jaw. Now Anne's nightmares and fear had come between them, shutting her out of part of his life.

The runway became a place, not a view, when the wheels touched down. Daniel ran forward to the plane and helped her to the slush-covered gravel. Thomas shrugged on his camel-hair topcoat and climbed out of the plane behind her. The pilot, an employee of Thomas's companies, opened the baggage compartment and unloaded.

"Dad, Anne. How was the flight?"

Anne caught the tension in his voice, too.

"What's wrong?" Thomas said, searching his son's face with worried eyes.

"Can I talk to you—"

"I'll wait inside," Anne said.

A shovelled walkway led from the landing strip to the terminal. Inside, Anne waited at the window that overlooked the field. Daniel and his father talked, hugged, and came inside the building to where she waited.

Thomas said, "Danny, can you put the bags in the car."

He put his arm around Anne. She caught the scent of his shaving cream, a subtle lemon, and something else, perhaps from the wool of his coat.

"Things aren't good at the house. Mom's memory is deteriorating, and she's easily confused. Daniel says the girls think it's a bad idea to bring a stranger, you, to stay, especially at Christmas."

"A stranger? But Thomas, your mother and I—"

"Yes, I know. She likes, liked you."

"What do you—"

Again, Anne watched his jaw work before he went on.

"I met both their husbands at Christmas, in that house, with my mother. I hate to ask you—"

"I'll call Catherine."

Why would they be so confrontational with him? What did their anger mean for her relationship with Thomas? Daniel had warm feelings towards her, but the girls, Claire and Cecilia, she didn't know. Wouldn't they take their attitude from their grandmother? Was all the warmth she had shown Anne, false? She waited for Catherine to answer her call and arranged to stay with her. She walked back to the terminal door where Thomas waited for her.

"She's going to Canada for a few days, but she says I can stay as long as I like."

"I'm sorry. I'll talk to the girls."

He took her in his arms, but she pushed out of his embrace.

"You'll have to see what's going on. I won't come where I'm not welcome."

Anne climbed into the back seat of the car, sliding a little on the smooth leather, and buckled her seatbelt. Thomas sat beside Daniel.

"Take us to Catherine's in town," he said.

"Dad, the girls are unreasonable. You talk—"

"Anne's decision."

Daniel put the car in gear and drove.

~

Catherine's Bed and Breakfast. Est.1983 asserted the little folk-art sign in front of the rambling, grey clapboard house. Catherine or one of the boys had painted the white picket fence surrounding the house since her last visit. Daniel took the bags to the porch and waited in the car for Thomas.

"I'll speak to the girls," Thomas said.

"Perhaps you should have done that before."

She cringed, hearing the nasty tone in her voice. He wasn't responsible for his daughters' attitudes.

"Anne—"

"Call me later. We can't talk about it until you know what's going on out there and how your mother is."

Thomas kissed her cheek and walked back to the car. She rang the doorbell.

Her friend, Catherine, swung the door wide and welcomed her in. Catherine's dark hair framed her oval face with its sharp nose and narrow jaw. Severity vanished with her charming smile. She was a Canadian who came down to marry Greg LaPlante, a man she met at her university. Greg liked fast cars and Canadian Rye as well as he liked Canadian women, a combination that killed him in the second year of their marriage, leaving her with twin boys, no money, an old house, and a lot of energy. The bed and breakfast fed, housed and clothed them ever since.

"Come in, come in," she said, hugging Anne.

Anne hung her parka and took off her boots before following Catherine into the bright-yellow kitchen, cheerful with botanical prints and windows that opened to bird feeders and a snow-shrouded garden. Chickadees and finches flitted from feeder to maple tree and back again, interrupted by the arrival of an aggressive nuthatch. Anne's eyes filled with tears and she stumbled into a press-back chair. Catherine busied herself with the kettle, until Anne wiped her eyes.

"Not the reception you expected? What's going on with Thomas?"

"Nothing with him. Something is wrong at the house. Perhaps his mother—"

"She's usually polite, if not always friendly."

"Yes, and gracious, to me. Thomas said she'd been vague."

Catherine put a porcelain mug, dotted with pink violets, in front of Anne. The fragrance of her favourite chai tea wafted up, soothing and familiar.

"Where is Maggie?" Anne asked, missing the grey, bushy-haired dog who was Catherine's companion. "She's not—"

"No, no," said Catherine. "We're going to be away and she's on vacation out at a friend's farm. She loves it there."

"I miss her comforting head on my knee."

"Comforting? What has happened since you were last here?"

"Spain."

"Yes?"

"I went to a village called Setenil de las Bodegas, for a rest after Bermuda. I was angry with Thomas and I couldn't sleep..."

"And then?"

"And then, I raced across Europe with a kidnapped Israeli child. At the end, a woman came to kill us and when she attacked me, the gun went off. I guess I pulled the trigger. I don't remember and then she was dead—"

Her words disappeared in wracking sobs. Catherine held her until her body relaxed.

"You were defending a child?"

"Yes."

"You had to."

"I didn't need to get involved at all. It's a world of spies, of Mossad and CIA and I got sucked in."

"To save a child?"

Catherine's eyes caught Anne's gaze and held on.

"To save a child?" she asked again.

"Yes. All my life I've hated guns and violence and now, twice, I fired a gun to protect myself. What does that make me?"

"Alive. And the child? Did he survive?"

"She. Yes. At night, I have nightmares of Esti's dead eyes."

"Esti was the woman in Spain?"

"Yes."

"Sometimes you must—"

Anne's hands gripped each other, her nails digging into her palms. She forced words out past the lump in her throat.

"Kill? I can't accept that."

"But—"

"I know. I did kill her and now Thomas can't confide in me because I'm too weak to help him."

"I doubt that. Tell me more about Spain."

Later, Anne sat reading in a comfortable chair in her room, near a window that overlooked the back garden. The words blurred and her mind ran in familiar grooves to the past. So many events had happened since she sat here for the first time several years before, after the death of her husband.

They had no children and she hoped carrying on in the routine of life would help her with her grief. It hadn't. Looking after so many children in her practice with behavioural and emotional problems took more than she had to give. She realized she was crawling through her days.

So, she retired. Her own doctor encouraged her to take a long leave, try a different life-style. She had no money worries. She and her husband both inherited wealth, in her case quite unexpectedly from a heretofore-unknown great-aunt. That discovery sparked her interest in genealogy and brought her to Culver's Mills the first time. Her discovery of a body in the library on her first visit had the unexpected consequence of bringing a host of new friends into her life. It also brought Thomas. And where was their relationship going?

She walked down to the library that doubled as Catherine's living room. The formal living and dining rooms served as a common room and a breakfast room for the B&B. Anne curled up in a chair upholstered in chintz, riotous with fantasy birds and flowers. She wrote a text to Thomas but decided not to send. No nuance in a text message. Too many opportunities for misunderstanding. She nodded over her book and drifted off to sleep.

~

Later that morning, Catherine stood in the doorway to the library wearing her navy winter coat and a jaunty red tuque.

"I'm sorry to leave you alone today, but I need to study for my torts exam."

"Torts?"

"Don't ask."

Catherine had decided on law school when her sons went to university and Anne had helped with the boys' school fees.

"I'll go for a walk," Anne said.

Since returning from Spain, she walked kilometres every day, hoping for the exhaustion that would leave her nights peaceful, hoping that she could lose herself in the landscape. Sometimes, it helped.

She paused at the bridge that spanned a weir, the water frozen now in fantastic shapes of white and green, and then strolled along a tree-lined street to the main square. The courthouse bounded the north side. The white-painted Methodist church dominated the south with rows of houses, stores, and offices in between. The whole thing was picture post-card Vermont, complete with Christmas lights in the trees and garlands circling the pillars in front of the courthouse. Paths led across the square, meeting at the heroic statue of the town founding-father in the middle. Anne passed it, rubbed the toe of one out-sized boot worn bright from years of others, hoped for a change in fortune and crossed to the other side to Erin's shop.

The building, dark grey granite on the outside, its interior lit with chandeliers and table lamps, was all dressed up for Christmas too. Erin decorated her shop in vignettes of rooms—a dining room with a mahogany sideboard and a table in the same rich wood, dressed with English china or a library with American Stickley furniture—all with festive touches like holly and silver bells.

The raised voices Anne heard when she opened the door didn't sound festive. She shut the door behind her. Three figures stood at the back of the shop, outside Erin's office, one a man who loomed over tiny Erin. They ignored the sound of the door chimes, intent on the conversation with Erin.

Usually, Anne dawdled for an hour looking at what treasures Erin had found, but the voices in the back rose and she rushed through the shop to the office.

"I told you," Erin said, "that a law firm sent me the jewels and that's where I'll return them."

The other person, a tall, fair woman moved in beside Erin, standing close, her voice harsh with menace. Her belted black leather coat evoked memories of agents in bad spy movies.

"They ours. Stolen from us in Russia and we want back."

Erin backed away from her but the door to her office behind her was closed.

"Erin, what's going on," Anne called.

The strangers turned venomous faces towards her and ran out, brushing her aside and sending her tumbling into a bookcase.

Erin guided Anne into a cream-coloured lady's chair and knelt beside her.

"Are you hurt?" she said.

"No, no. What was going on?"

"They think I have something that belongs to them."

"Why?"

"Let me get some tea."

For a few minutes, Erin busied herself at the table in a corner of her office where she kept a kettle. When she reappeared, she carried a tray with teapot and cups. She set one of the Stickley tables close to Anne and pulled a chair around for herself.

"I qualified as a gemologist last year. Did you know that?" When Anne shook her head, Erin went on. "I received a commission from a law firm to assess some jewellery and three figurines. Those people claim they are the true owners and want them back."

She poured a cup of tea for each of them and offered Anne a shortbread cookie, shaped like a Christmas tree decorated in red and green.

"Have they been in before?"

"No."

"Perhaps you should call the police or Adam."

Adam, Erin's fiancée, had until recently been the lead detective on the local police force but was now a final year law student.

Erin shook her head and leaned back in her chair.

"I'll talk to him later. He's in class. What would I say to the police? They didn't threaten me in so many words."

"They both had a nasty look, especially her. Will Adam be home tonight?"

"No, he's in Burlington for the week."

"Perhaps call him."

"He'd rush right back, and it's an important week at school for him."

"Be sure to set your security alarm."

"I will."

Anne stood up and walked across to the door to retrieve her parka. Erin helped her with a reluctant sleeve.

"Have you come for Christmas at the Beauchamps?" Erin said.

"I'm staying with Catherine for the moment but I may go out to there. It depends."

"Is something wrong?"

"I'm not sure. Tell Adam I'm sorry I missed him."

"He'll call you."

Anne left the shop, strolled along two sides of the square and back to Catherine's.

Chapter Two

A rapid knocking at her door woke Anne the next morning. At least, she thought it was morning. A narrow band of brightness fell across her bed from the space at the bottom of the window blind. She heard shallow gasps and knew she had shouted out in a nightmare. She struggled to sit up.

"Come in. It's all right. I was dreaming."

Catherine came in, wrapped in a green robe, trailing its cords behind her. She sat on the bed beside Anne and put her arm around her.

"What was it?"

Anne willed her breathing to slow, but still, she trembled. Her voice strained past the globe of fear in her throat.

"It's always the same. Esti is falling, and her dead eyes are staring at me. Asking why. Always asking why."

"Esti, the woman who was hunting you in Spain?"

"Yes."

"How often?"

"It was every night, but now only once a week or so. I think I'm getting better, or at least my nights are."

Better. Was she better? Perhaps, a little.

"You need some coffee."

Later, they sat in the kitchen, watching a golden dawn creep across the yard and through the windows, slanting sunshine across the table, scattering colour from a ruby vase. She touched the white petals of the mums it contained.

"Have you seen someone about the nightmares?"

"Yes. A psychologist. PTSD, he said. Mild. Those poor souls who have severe, I can't imagine what they suffer, if this is mild. And he sent me on to a therapist called Andrea. I still work with her."

"Does Thomas know?"

Anne's fingers beat a frantic tattoo on the tabletop. She flattened them, willing them to behave, but they thumped away, in spite of her.

"Oh yes. He's not part of my problem; I'm part of his. He's coming this morning, and we're going out to the house. He wants me to guide him about his mother. But the girls—"

Catherine reached across the table and settled Anne's writhing fingers.

"Do they know you? I remember them as being quite pleasant."

"No, they don't. We've not met, so the girls only know what their grandmother or Thomas have told them. Perhaps her courtesy hid dislike."

"I can't imagine that, and they will at least be polite."

"Yes, politely rejecting and then, what?"

"Trust Thomas."

Anne pushed back her chair and paced the kitchen. Tears coursed down her cheeks. She brushed them away and stood at the window. Catherine poured more coffee.

"What if it comes down his children or me? It won't be me. I won't let it be me."

"You would give him up?"

"I wouldn't let him give up his family for me."

She collapsed in her chair and leaned forward, gripping her hands until the knuckles blanched.

"They are adults, Anne, not teenage children. It won't come to that."

"You think I'm over-reacting?"

"What's that you like to say? You need more data."

"I'll get that today, when Thomas takes me out there."

"In the meantime, how about breakfast?"

∾

Later that morning, Thomas arrived to pick up Anne. She and Catherine sat in the Adirondack chairs on the porch, wrapped in blankets, chatting. Thomas opened the gate in the picket fence and bounded up the stairs. He was heir to the Beauchamp fortune, a businessman, and a world-class skier as a young man, a lithe and tanned fifty-something, not tall, with brown eyes and a prominent nose. He bent over to kiss Catherine's cheek and turned to give Anne a quick embrace. His dark eyes smiled into hers.

"Okay this morning?"

"Dreams again, but okay now. Have all the family arrived?"

"Daniel's wife is coming later this week, but Claire's husband is in the reserve and called up."

"Deployed?"

"Not yet."

They drove out to his home, with its granite walls settled in the land his ancestors had occupied for three hundred years. Tall windows flanked the robin's egg blue front door, but Thomas drove around to the back, and they entered through the kitchen, too large now for a house that was home to one most of the time. A woman in a white apron stood at the stove.

Thomas said good morning and asked where everyone was.

"Still in the dining room," the cook said and turned back to her omelette pan.

Anne had been to the house before and had noticed the art and architecture. The interior decorating showed two hands at work, or maybe three. The walls were painted light colours, but the furniture comprised American antiques of the eighteenth and early nine-teenth centuries. Those were Madame Beauchamp's taste, Anne knew. On the other hand, the art was solidly twentieth-century, some representational, some not. Anne's favourite was a Canadian painting, by Beaver Hall artist, Kathleen Morris, a vivid market scene in Ottawa, bought by Thomas, she suspected, or perhaps Claire, his art student daughter, now a busy mother of twins. There had been a few additions, however. A pair of religious paintings, depicting the biblical miracle of the loaves and fishes hung on the staircase wall. Madame Beauchamp's taste, not Claire's, she thought.

Thomas's mother, wearing a dark burgundy sweater over a cream silk blouse, presided at the head of the mahogany table in the dining room. The crystal and silver gleamed, set off against the dark wood of the table, dressed only with linen placemats for this, the first and most casual meal of the day in her formal house. Thomas's daughters flanked her, and her grandson sat on one side at the other end. Thomas took Anne to his mother.

"Mom, this is my friend, Anne. You met her last year."

Her frail hand, its back blue-veined and mottled, extended long elegant fingers to grasp hers. Her dark eyes, the irises blurred with age, looked into hers with no sign of recognition.

"Did I, dear? It must have slipped my mind. Do sit down, Anne. Would you like some breakfast?"

"No, thank you, Madame Beauchamp."

Daniel got up to come to Anne and give her a two-cheek kiss. Thomas introduced his daughters, Claire and Cecilia, twins, both blonde with dark eyes. They spoke in unison.

"Dad, I thought we agreed—" said Claire.

"How could you?" Cecilia said.

Thomas glared them into silence.

"Not now. Where are the children?"

"They ate in the kitchen with Alison. And now they are all napping."

"Thomas," his mother said, "Your children are so good; they've gone right to sleep. Who are all these charming people?"

The girls gasped and Claire, ashen, mumbled an excuse and ran from the table.

"Mom, perhaps you are tired and would like to sit in the study for a short time. Daniel and Anne and I have some business to discuss. Would you help her please, Cecilia?"

This was a Thomas Anne hadn't seen before, in charge of his family and obeyed even when the girls were furious.

When they left, Daniel said, "You see how it is, Dad. The girls are shocked every time something like that happens, and they blame everything but a disease. It will be Anne this time, confusing mother."

"It likely was me," Anne said. "Unfamiliar face, confusing her and forcing her to process. I should leave and let your family come to terms with this. She needs assessment."

She looked down the table to Daniel.

"She said no doctors to Cecilia this morning," Daniel said.

"At some level, she knows something is wrong, and she's frightened. Try to get her to see someone. Could you take me back to town," she said, turning to Thomas.

"Would you mind driving yourself. I should stay here."

Drive herself? Of course, she could, but if this was how it was to be, banished from his home because of the girls' attitude, perhaps she should book a flight home.

She waited inside the door until Thomas brought around a red Toyota.

"Whose is this?" she said.

"Mom's."

"She won't—"

"She doesn't remember about the car. Years ago, she was driven everywhere by a chauffeur, and she thinks that is how it is now."

"Oh, Thomas. Please call me."

When she turned onto the highway, she glanced in the rear-view mirror. Thomas was still on the porch, watching.

Chapter Three

The stone house disappeared from her mirror. Anne drove past pastures outlined by white horse fences and sedate mansions sheltered in their grounds, pristine under their blanket of snow. In the summer, the lawns swept down to the road and horses grazed in the fields. This was Thomas's world. It couldn't be hers. Not ever. Not with his family's attitude. She yearned for the quiet streets of her village in Ontario and her granite bungalow. Perhaps she was meant to be alone, to have only these occasional times when she became part of a couple again. If Michael hadn't died, what direction would their lives have taken together? She gave herself a mental shake. What ifs were a waste of time and only brought on more longing for what might have been.

Should she go home? Perhaps. What was the matter with those girls? Why didn't they want Thomas to be happy? She pounded the steering wheel and tears blurred her vision. She slowed the car and stopped on the shoulder of the road, waiting for the tears to end, for the anger to fade.

Back in town and not wanting to be alone with her thoughts, at least not yet, about what had happened at the Beauchamps, Anne parked near the square and walked to Lil's Diner.

Thomas told her that the restaurant occupying the corner opposite to Erin's shop, was there when he was young. At the top of three cement stairs, the door opened to an old-fashioned diner with a long white enamel counter facing the entrance. The sweet and savoury aroma of maple-smoked bacon mixed with that of the French fries a gaggle of teenaged girls shared. Late breakfasters and early lunchers filled the line of red stools and the booths upholstered in black faux leather. Anne found space at the end of the row, overlooking the square. An antique milkshake machine stood next to an espresso maker with all its levers and switches that steamed and huffed at the end of the counter. The owner, Peg, often took the morning shift at the cash register but not today. The waiter, a woman Anne had met before, told her that Peg took her sister to Burlington once a week for a new therapy for her arthritis.

Anne's seat faced the door and overlooked the other diners. She munched on her western sandwich for a few minutes, leafing through the local paper. When the waiter arrived with more coffee, she noticed a man sitting with his back to her, two booths closer to the door. He must have come in while she was absorbed in the local news. Black, he stood out in the restaurant of white patrons and waiters. Something about his back, the set of his shoulders, the shape of his head, and his close-cropped, greying hair was familiar to her. The waiter reached him with the coffee pot, he turned his head, and she knew.

Quin, CIA, a former colleague of Thomas, a man who saved her sister's life in Bermuda and helped her in Spain. What was he doing in Culver's Mills? It must be Thomas. What did he want of Thomas who promised he would resign as an asset to the CIA, promised he was a businessman and only a businessman? Had he lied to her; told her what she needed to hear. She felt her throat close in her old reaction to stress. She left money on the table and rushed down the aisle to the door before panic set in. On the street, she stopped and managed her breathing and forced herself to stroll towards her car. Behind her, she heard Lil's door open.

~

Anne hurried towards the car she'd parked near the old mill over-looking the pond and the weir. She heard footfalls behind her. She fumbled at the door but swung around when the follower said her name. Quin, tall, black, handsome with an engaging smile and a calm voice, sometimes with a Jamaican accent, but today, solidly New York, spoke to her.

"Anne. It's Quin. Why are you running away from me?"

Anne searched the brown eyes. What were they hiding? What did he want with her or with Thomas?

"Why are you here? Thomas—"

"Nothing to do with Tom."

"He promised—"

"He told me. But I need you to do something for me."

She knew it. If Quin were in Culver's Mills, it meant she and perhaps Thomas, certainly Thomas, would be drawn into his shadow world again. She wouldn't do it. Whatever it was? She stepped back from him and took a breath.

"Me? Why?"

His brows knitted over his broad nose as his eyes questioned her.

"Because you know who I am and I don't want anyone else to. I need you to keep that to yourself."

Keep his identity quiet? Of course, she could. Anne nodded her head but frowned up into Quin's face.

"What about Thomas? If he sees you—"

"Tell him I'm here and what I said."

"Sure, and then, when you talk with him, you'll have something for him to do or be in some trouble and need his help. Can't you leave him alone?"

"I've told you my being here has nothing to do with him."

"But what—"

"That's all, Anne. All I can or will tell you. Will you do this for me?"

"Yes, but—"

"All I need."

Quin walked away and disappeared behind the mill. Anne sat in her car, found her hands shaking and concentrated on her breathing until the turmoil inside settled. She drove away, towards Catherine's. Maybe, she thought, she'd pick up her clothes and keep on going, drive away from Culver's Mills and across the border.

Except this wasn't her car. She laughed at the absurdity of plotting an escape in a borrowed car. But was that what her relationship with Thomas was, a trap? She drove on, back to Catherine's.

≈

The woman exited the flight from JFK airport in New York and picked up the rental car at the line of desks near the baggage carousel. Tall, with her dark hair brushing the shoulders of her long navy wool coat, she drew glances as she left the reservation desk. The car, a blue Chevrolet Cruze, waited at the end of a covered walkway to the parking garage. At least this airport was civilized, she thought, protected from the northern weather. How tired she was of cold. Much as she loved to ski, this would be the last winter without the warmth of the sun. But first, she had to carry out this absurd mission for the Russian.

She tossed her hat and gloves on the seat beside her and drove to a storage facility on the outskirts of Burlington, opened the unit and checked the firearms she found waiting for her. At least they were her choices.

She followed the GPS instructions to an inn on a lake near the town of Culver's Mills, Vermont. There, Alexei had assured her, she would find the objects she sought in an antique store. Easy, he said. He sent those bumbling Russians ahead of her, to gather information about the shop and the woman who ran it.

The GPS steered her left off the highway and down a long lane, overhung with tall, leafless trees, to the shore of a lake. The building, painted white, faded into the winter landscape, marked only by dark green shutters and a double door of bright red.

Her phone buzzed as she tipped the bellboy. Ivan.

"So you have arrived?"

"Yes. You found the shop?"

"Yes. We will visit it this afternoon, and then we can all go home."

"Perhaps. Don't underestimate these people, Ivan."

"A woman running an antique store in a village? You are joking. We will have the jewels by tonight."

"Check with me later."

"Da."

Fools. Why did Alexei insist on them? She must be careful. Perhaps the idea was that after they recovered the jewels, she would be expendable? Absurd, but she would take care. She loaded the small pistol with its efficient silencer. She would be ready.

Chapter Four

The kitchen door slammed behind her. Catherine swivelled from the stove when Anne thumped into a chair at the table.

"What's happened?"

"I had to leave the Beauchamps."

"Why? Did Thomas—"

"Nothing. He did nothing unless you count not insisting to his daughters that his life is his own. I suppose that's not fair either. I chose to go, but the girls are upset. It's clear their grandmother is dementing, but they're blaming me for bringing confusion into her life. At lunch, she didn't know who they were."

Anne passed her hands over her face and her teeth clenched.

"As bad as that?"

"For that half-hour. I expect it was me, confusing the poor soul and I said so and left."

"And Thomas?"

"He loaned me a car."

The arrogance of it. He loaned her a car. But was it arrogant? Would she have abandoned her dementing mother at that moment?

"He didn't drive you?"

"No. And I've no idea when I'll see him again."

"I'm sure he'll call you when he has taken care of the situation. After all, you still have his car. Lunch?"

"I stopped at Lil's. I'm going to nap, or try to."

"Tea?"

"No, thanks. Yes, I will. I'll take it up with me."

Hours later, Anne woke, lost for a moment in the unfamiliar room. Down the stairs, she found Catherine in the kitchen, law books spread out on the table, her fingers flying over the keyboard of her computer.

"You must have had a good nap. No bad dreams?"

"None that I remember."

"Would you like to go out for dinner to Evan's?"

"Do Mary and Andre still own it?

Historical treasures, long-hidden but discovered when Anne helped unmask a murderer, gave the two, a local girl and a French chef, enough money to give up the restaurant business forever. They'd become friends.

"Yes. Andre says all he wants to do is cook."

"I'd love to see them again."

"Not this time, I'm afraid. They're in France for Christmas."

"Who is in the kitchen?"

"That's a surprise."

Two hours later, they paused in the foyer of Evan's. A mirror above a flower-painted console table reflected the glow of a ruby-glass shaded lamp and spilled hues of red-gold across the oriental carpet. They followed the waiter, past tables set with cream dinnerware atop deep-red tablecloths and royal blue napkins. A brick fireplace dominated one end of the room, surrounded by a wall of mahogany panels, punctuated on one side by a wood storage area and the other by a glass-fronted, mahogany bookcase. Their table occupied a bow window, its dark blue drapes shutting out the black night.

Anne's chair gave her a view of the restaurant and its other patrons, Catherine's only of Anne and the books behind her.

"Would you prefer to sit here?" Anne asked.

"Not at all."

A drift of perfume caught Anne's attention. Subtle and French, she thought. Expensive for a weeknight out in Culver's Mills. Likely the woman seated at a table for one, behind Catherine, was the source. The woman's head jerked forward. Her shoulder-length dark hair framed a long narrow face. Her eyes were slightly slanted, giving her a Eurasian look. Also, very French, Anne thought, from the impeccable twist on the silk scarf to her meticulous manicure and flawless nail polish the colour of vintage claret.

"What is it?"

"Later. Tell me about the boys."

Catherine soon engulfed her in tales of her twins and their first semester at college. While Anne listened, she watched the woman at the next table who now ignored her and everyone else in the room, concentrating on her cell phone as though reading a book. Perhaps she was, Anne thought. But a woman like that, alone in Culver's Mills? Perhaps she had something to do with Quin's mission? Nothing to do with her. She concentrated on Catherine's stories.

"There's a Christmas open house tour," Catherine said. "Would you like to go tomorrow?"

"This close to Christmas? Brave people."

"Only seven homes. The garden society again, raising money for the parks."

"If I have time, I'd love to."

"I'll call about tickets. The Culver's house is on it."

Anne had met the Culvers, one of the founding families, along with the Beauchamps when she visited Culver's Mills for the first time.

"Do they dress it for the holidays?"

"Oh, yes."

"So, who is in the kitchen?" Anne asked at the end of the meal. "My fish was delicious."

"Dylan."

"No!"

Dylan was a young man on a dangerous path when he discovered cooking and was sent to school. Arriving from the kitchen, so tall his chef's cap almost touched the ceiling in the eighteenth-century room, he made his rounds, stopping at their table to greet Anne and Catherine before passing on to the next, the one with the exotic woman.

After a curt word with the chef, the woman, her gait that of a high-fashion model, strutted her way across the room to the foyer and retrieved her coat and gloves. Before she left, she glanced into the room. Anne looked away.

"Now who could she be?" Anne said.

"Who?"

"The woman with the expensive perfume. She's gone now. You didn't notice her?"

"No."

"Interesting."

"Sometimes you wonder a little too much."

Anne laughed, and Catherine and she got up to leave.

Colette caught the eye of the woman at the next table and in that instant, she knew. She recognized the McPhail woman, the one who interfered with her plans in Bermuda and Spain. She dropped her gaze to her cell phone, searched her database for the photo of the woman and her dossier and stayed engrossed in it until her dinner arrived. McPhail wouldn't recognize her. None of the agencies had a photo of her. But what about those two she hired to help her? She didn't want to hire Russians; she didn't like to work with them but her employer forced them on her. Damned Alexei. If he wanted her to do the job, he should have left it to her. Her stomach knotted. She pushed her food around on her plate and forced herself to pick at it. The chicken was well-cooked and if she didn't eat it, people, that waiter perhaps, would remember her.

At her meal's end, after the chef with his ludicrous hat made his rounds, she paid and left. Was the woman watching her? She paused to inspect her face in the foyer mirror and glanced back into the room. McPhail's head bobbed down. Recognition? Perhaps, but how?

Her rental car, a generic brand that would blend in with all the others, sat in the parking lot, already covered in snow. Snow in Switzerland, when she watched it from her penthouse was one thing, but here, in the country, filling the roadways and blinding her when she drove, quite another. She'd have to call Alexei and tell him about McPhail.

The car lights picked out the entrance to the inn she chose, a converted white clapboard mansion, large enough that it would be comfortable, and expensive enough that privacy was part of the package. French voices carried to her as she strolled across the lobby. Dialect French, likely from Canada, she thought. She rode the narrow elevator to her third-floor suite.

The door opened to a comfortable space, with room enough for a four-poster bed, covered with an antique cream-coloured quilt. A fireplace with a mantel in the same cream stood below a painting of an old mill. Oddly for a hotel, the work was a genuine oil, but likely a local artist. Well-done, however. She crossed the room to the Queen Anne desk set against the wall and checked the phone. No messages, but then Alexei wouldn't call her on an insecure line. She flicked on the gas fireplace, enjoying the flames swirling above the artificial logs. She typed the number in Moscow on the satellite phone Alexei had given her.

"Da?"

"Colette. There is a complication."

She paused. Now that he was on the phone, should she tell him? She must.

"And?"

"The woman who caused me so much trouble in Bermuda and Spain is here."

"There. You mean in that small town?"

"Yes, here."

"Is she tracking you?"

"I do not think so. No one knows what I look like. All my previous work was strictly phone and computer. I told you I was the incorrect person for this."

"You are the perfect person for this. Don't let your personal feelings about this woman interfere in the job. Recovering the Fabergé is all that matters. We will not hesitate to punish failure."

Colette drummed her fingers silently on the desk. McPhail would not obstruct her this time. Not again.

"You know that, Colette?"

"Yes."

"Good. Do not draw attention to yourself. How did Dasha and Ivan do?"

"They haven't checked in as yet."

"See that they keep you informed."

Now she heard the empty silence of a dropped call. Dasha and Ivan. Dunderheads. Why did Alexei insist on them? Why did he insist on her? How she hated working with Russians, but Alexei had evidence, he said, evidence of her work with the cartel, evidence he would send to Interpol if she didn't. Worse, he knew where she was.

She texted Ivan, asking if he had the goods. He replied that they hadn't been able to get them from the woman by the method she suggested and now Alexei would blame them. *What now*, he texted. *Do nothing*, she replied, *until tomorrow*.

Nothing for them until tomorrow, but tonight she would have a quiet look around that antique shop.

The flames from the gas fireplace leapt and chased each other across the simulated logs. How long before she could return to her private life, escape from this hell and live in her house in the sheltered village in France? How long and at what cost?

She dozed until her alarm woke her and it was time to visit the antique shop. Perhaps it would be all over tonight, and she could leave.

~

Ivan parked the van in front of unit five. What a mess, he thought. They had painted over rust, and already stains showed through; new shingles but the surface of the stucco was peeling near the downspouts. And the snow. Day after day. They might as well be in Siberia again. Inside, they ate a pizza and drank a litre of wine. At least the wine from California was good.

Later, curled beside Dasha, he drifted into sleep until the sharp jangle from his cell phone roused him. He moaned and rolled away from her to read his text, swore, and tossed the phone on the bed between them.

"What?"

"That bitch. Do nothing, she says. Wait for her instructions."

Dasha read the message on the phone and snorted. Her green eyes, slanted over high cheekbones squinted at the screen.

"Do you want me to answer?"

"No. But I want to do something."

Dasha, her blonde hair tumbled after their evening in bed, slithered off and pulled a robe around her.

"What?" she said at the bathroom door.

"Do the job our way? The lock is simple, and so is the security. The code is easily broken."

"You think she keeps the jewels in the shop?"

"Or where she lives, upstairs."

"How do you know where she lives?"

"Yesterday, when I went out, I watched the shop when she closed. She came out and went to a door at the side. The lights came on upstairs."

"I'm going to shower. Tell me what to do after."

Shower. They could get millions, and she has to shower. He leaned back against the thin pillows and planned.

27

"So?" she said, standing naked in the doorway.

"We'll go tonight. But now we have time."

Later, they dressed in dark jeans and black jackets and waited until 11:00 pm.

"What if we have to go upstairs? Will you kill her?"

"No. If the egg isn't there, the antique store woman has hidden it and we need her alive to tell us."

"Afterwards?"

"It depends."

An hour later, the lock opened, and Ivan and Dash entered the shop. A few minutes search stretched into twenty and still no jewels. A sound from the back alerted Ivan.

"Someone's coming."

Dasha melted back into the shadows, and Ivan stood beside the desk. His hand closed on a paperweight.

Chapter Five

At midnight, Colette changed into a dark hoodie and black jeans, pocketed her set of keys and picks and at the last moment, her gun, and left the hotel, driving through a frozen landscape towards the town. Above her, more stars than she had seen since her last visit to the mountains spread across the black sky. No moon. A good night for reconnaissance. She parked close to the mill park. The subject of the painting in her room, a stone building, loomed over the pond.

The streets were empty; the town asleep like the village in the Dordogne where she owned a cottage. When she returned to France, not as Colette but as the absentee owner, she would retire. She had enough to live on. But the Russians. If she were lucky, they might want to use her again, and if she failed, they would kill her. Her stomach churned and a chill spread through her.

She slipped along a path through the path and along a street to the town square. Christmas lights, hanging in long, white ropes across the square and outlining branches in the trees, cast a pale light on the snow around the statue of the founding father. Beyond, the antique store lay in darkness, and better, the apartment lights were off too. She hurried past the parking lot on one side of the building to the back. The alarm wasn't set. Careless but who would expect thieves in this little town.

Inside, she waited for her eyes to adjust. The tiny flashlight she carried cast a thin beam that danced around the storage area. This was not a high-security jewellery firm but a one-owner shop. The woman likely didn't have a safe. Where would she keep valuable items? Colette moved into the front room and saw her light reflected from a glass-fronted case. Locked. The owner wasn't expecting to be robbed. Behind the glass lay pendants, rings, and an enamelled brooch inset with diamonds. Nothing much, she thought, but there were drawers beneath.

A random noise from the rear brought her around. She pulled her gun, small but fitted with an efficient silencer, from her pocket. Her light picked out Ivan's face, cadaveric in the deep shadows. Behind him, his partner pushed him on.

"What are you doing here?" Ivan said, his voice hoarse.

"Looking around. You? Why didn't you check with me? Breaking in here was not part of the plan for you."

Dasha's voice came from the darkness.

"Why should we do as you say? You said it would be easy. Scare the little girl who owns the shop. Her friend arrives, and she's not scared."

Colette sensed rather than saw her moving away from Ivan and circling her. What was she up to?

"Dasha?" Ivan said.

"There are some expensive items here, locked in these foolish cases. We should take them."

Colette backed towards the case.

"No. I forbid it."

"You can't forbid it. You hired us to find Russian jewels. Russian. They belong to us, to our country, not to you."

"Dasha, stop," Ivan said.

"She thinks she can order us around. I don't let any weak French woman order me around."

What was wrong with her, Colette wondered. Soon she would wake the woman upstairs.

"We have to get out of here before the woman hears us." Ivan said.

"No. I want these jewels. Get out of my way."

Colette saw the flash of a knife in the other woman's hand as she lunged towards her. Colette's arm came up; Dasha's eyes opened wide, she mouthed something, a word. The body crashed to the floor; a black hole in the centre of the forehead oozed blood.

"What have you done?"

Ivan rushed towards them but reeled back when Colette pointed her pistol at him. He dropped the paperweight he still held.

"Get out of here."

"Maybe she's not dead."

"She's dead. Go. Ahead of me."

She gestured towards the back of the shop. Ivan stumbled away, found his footing and ran from the building. Colette followed and left the door open. Ivan's van raced past her.

She forced herself to stroll across the square and along the street to her car. Her shaking hand missed the ignition. She fought for control, to keep down the vomit that threatened. She'd killed her. She'd never done that before. All that training and not once. A few minutes later, she drove out of the town towards her hotel.

Colette parked the car close to the entrance to the inn, crossed the now-silent lobby and climbed the stairs to her floor. Once inside, she leaned back against the door. Her heart still pounded in her chest, in her ears. What to do? If she left now, when the news broke the manager might notify the police about the strange guest who disappeared in the middle of the night. She couldn't do that. Better to check out in the morning. She prowled the room, pulled the drapes and stood at the window. Snow drifted across the parking lot, covering the cars.

She switched on the fire, drew up a wingback chair, sat, and closed her eyes. Dasha's face appeared, mouthing that word. What had she said? Did she say no? Ivan, that's what she said. She called for her husband, and she died. What would she have said, in the end, if Dasha had killed her? Her child's name? Or would she call for her mother, dead long years ago?

She reconstructed the scene in the antique store. Why were they there? Fools. Fighting with the owner in front of a witness and breaking in at night. The police would be told and on Ivan's trail. If he were caught, would he give her up? He would want to, because of Dasha, but he was afraid of Alexei, too.

She leaned forward in the chair and held her cold hands to the fire. She was still shaking. Why? Dasha tried to kill her. She had a knife and she was mad. She would have killed her or slashed her face or blinded her. She knew Russians. She would tell Alexei that she defended herself against the madwoman. His people, foisted on her, his responsibility. She told him she worked better alone. What would he do? Would he call off the operation and send someone else? But that someone would kill her. What if she left and fled across the border to Canada and on to Europe. No one suspected her. No one would follow. Except for Alexei.

She filled a glass from the tap in the kitchen with water, added a measure of whiskey and went back to the window. Why was the landscape so visible? It was always so when it snowed. She could drive into that landscape and disappear, lost to Alexei and to Ivan. Ivan didn't worry her. A bungler if ever there was one.

She cranked the lever on the window. The cold crept into the room, into her bones. Snow swirled across the lintel and fell in gentle heaps on the carpet. She closed it and collapsed into the chair by the fire. She would disappear.

But then she remembered. That woman, that McPhail, she saw her at the restaurant. Maybe McPhail did know what she looked like. She worked with Mossad. Maybe they shared a photo with McPhail. For that matter, how had Alexei found her? She had to get rid of that woman before she sent the FBI or maybe the CIA after her. Tomorrow she would leave, drive to that city, Burlington, and wait and plan. For now, she would sleep. She could sleep. It wasn't her fault. The woman attacked her. She would sleep.

~

The white van roared away from the antique store. No sign of the woman who entered the shop with the driver. And where the hell was Colette? Quin slipped along the street and into the alley behind Erin's store. The door stood open. Beyond, he saw the crumpled figure of the woman. He stepped across the few meters that separated them. Not Colette. A kill shot in the centre of the forehead. He didn't touch her, but wheeled and ran, leaving nothing behind.

Where had Colette gone? A blue car turned at the corner of the square on a road that led out to a country inn. He drove through the snow until he was opposite the building. Only luck had brought him to check in at the same place she chose to stay. Better lucky than smart.

The blue Chevy angled into a parking spot near the front entrance. A single guest room showed a light, and that cut out, leaving the facade black. Inside, behind the reception desk, a man leaned forward, his face a flickering mask of colours from the television he watched.

Had he been seen at the antique store? He drove back to town, past the entrance to the square, expecting police cars and an ambulance but the square slept too.

Should he make an anonymous call, describing the van and the car? From where? Not his cell and there was nothing open but a Tim Horton out on the highway, where asking would draw attention to him, and he wasn't supposed to be here. He was supposed to be in France, tracking Colette. He was supposed to have handed the investigation to the FBI if it brought him back to the USA.

He picked up a coffee, swung back around to the inn and went up to his room. He'd see Colette at breakfast.

Chapter Six

Early the next morning, Anne crept down to the kitchen without waking Catherine and brewed some coffee. Another restless night, but no nightmares, no dreams of a dead woman accusing her interrupted her sleep. She needed to walk as she did most mornings now, kilometres at a time, filling her mind with images of the landscape.

She crossed the bridge and ploughed through the fresh snow to the square and across to Erin's shop. Erin's window, changed for the season, today featured a festive holiday table set with brown transferware. Anne peered through the window, past the display at something out-of-place at the back. What was lying there? The morning sun slanted into the darkened antique store and through a crystal chandelier, cascading a rainbow of colours over a shape huddled on the floor near the glass cases. Beyond, the back door stood ajar. Anne quelled the thought that she should walk on, leaving trouble to be found by someone else this time. What if it was Erin, ill or injured?

She hurried around the building, past the door to Erin's loft, to the back of the building. Two cars, one of them Erin's battered red van, pointed nose-out into the lane. Past them, a loading door opened into the storage area. Anne stepped through and waited for her eyes to adjust to the light.

Oh no, not again, she thought. The shape resolved into a woman, lying face down on the chestnut floorboards. Anne touched the hand with the back of hers and felt the cold of the long-dead. She searched for a pulse in the carotid artery, but it was hopeless.

Anne slumped against the edge of a crate, a few metres from the young woman's body. A single dark hole pierced the white skin of the forehead above the eyes. Her head had fallen to the left as she died and a trickle of blood had oozed from the wound, coursed into the left ear and out, and congealed on the floor where she lay. On the wall behind, a spray of blood and brain traced a pattern. Anne touched the face with the back of her hand. Cold. She sought a pulse in the thin neck but found nothing and turned away from the clouded blue eyes.

She dialled 911 and went back in and sat. So, young, she thought. Her hands trembled. What was this? She'd seen the dead before. Not so often in her life, paediatricians didn't, but lately... She wanted to be sure, to touch the young woman again, but she knew she shouldn't. No way to explain why she would do that. She gripped her hands, fought down nausea.

Three bodies in as many years. Would they be suspicious of her this time? That happened before, in Bermuda. In the distance, she heard the sirens.

She rubbed her hands on the soft fabric of her pale blue parka and shivered, cold in spite of her warm coat. Silence flowed from the body on the floor and surrounded her, until it was broken by the wail of sirens. Could she face the questions alone? No, not again. She punched in Thomas's number on her cell phone.

She punched in Thomas's number on her cell phone.

"Thomas, I'm at Erin's. There's a body—"

"Erin?"

"No. The police are coming."

"I'll be right there."

She walked out of the building and pushed Erin's doorbell.

"Who is it?"

"Erin, it's Anne McPhail—"

"You're early—"

"Is Adam there? You both should come down. Something's happened down here."

"No, he's in Burlington. But what—"

"Get dressed, Erin. The police are coming."

"The police. Why?"

"Here they are."

A dark blue, unmarked vehicle, identified by its red flashing light, threw up mounds of brown slush in the road before it stopped beside Erin's van. Anne recognized the man who climbed out. Pete Graham, a sergeant when she was last in Culver's Mills, now a detective lieutenant. He took Adam's old job, Catherine told her, when they were catching up last evening after she arrived at the B&B.

The stocky figure walked over, his hand outstretched to shake hers. His forehead wrinkled in a quizzical frown.

"Again, Anne? Damn shame you have to find a body every time you arrive."

"I wouldn't choose it, Pete."

She shook his hand and waited.

"Touch her?"

"I felt her hand with the back of mine and for a pulse in her neck, left side. I don't think I touched anything else in there."

"Tell Erin?"

"She'll be down. I didn't say what I found."

Pete nodded. He'd shaved his head since she was last in Culver's Mills, perhaps because it was thinning a bit on top, and he wore a gold band on his left hand. Catherine didn't tell her he had married. Erin came around the corner.

Erin Maxwell, engaged to Adam Davidson, Pete's old boss, now finishing his law degree, owned the antique store and lived above. A petite brunette, she wore a navy sweatshirt and faded jeans covered by a puffy red vest, her dark eyes enormous in the pale oval of her face.

"Morning, Erin," Pete said, shaking her hand.

"Morning. What's happened? Why did you call the police, Anne?"

"Come with me but brace yourself. It's bad, Erin," Pete said.

Pete walked her in and a few minutes later, back out. Anne put her arm around the younger woman and sat her down on the side of the loading dock. Her face, drained of colour, had the deer-in-the-headlights look people had after a severe shock.

"Know her?" Pete asked.

Erin nodded her head.

"I think so."

Her voice cracked with strain, and she tried again.

"I think she was one of a couple who wanted me to give them some jewels that were sent for assessment. But it was a commission from an estate, so I said no. They were upset."

"How upset?"

"Quite."

"I saw them too," Anne said. "They were looming over Erin when I came in. He looked enraged and dangerous to me, and she looked almost out of control."

"The jewels? Expensive?"

"Yes, by ordinary standards, anyway. Those people said they descended from Russian nobility and the jewels are Fabergé."

"Explain that later. Wait upstairs, okay? You, too, Anne."

Anne and Erin climbed the stairs to her loft.

Upstairs, the door opened to a scene from Edwardian times. The space, undivided except for a bedroom and bathroom, overlooked the square from the tall front windows. Erin often redecorated, moving pieces between the loft and the store. The current selection included a sofa and two Bergère chairs with caned backs and arms.

The chairs, their seats upholstered in soft navy velvet with white piping sat on an antique Persian rug, glorious in vibrant blues and reds.

A polished wood chandelier with four globes of greenish glass hung above a round mahogany table with scrolled legs that tapered to brass lions' feet. Four matching chairs, their black leather seats worn by decades of use, surrounded it.

"How charming," Anne said. "May I make some tea?"

"Yes,"

Erin waved blindly towards the kitchen. She sat back in one of the chairs and closed her eyes, but when Anne returned with the tea, she was moving a painting back into place.

"The jewellery?"

"All here."

Anne poured the tea, insisting over Erin's objections that she needed sugar for the shock. So did she, she thought, as the teapot chittered against the cup. What could they talk about that didn't include the body lying on the cement floor below?

"What are those?" she said, pointing to some objects on a pie-crust table, misshapen and out-of-place in their elegant surroundings.

"The law firm sent those too. They insisted some avant-garde artist sculpted them, but I haven't found any reference as yet."

So much for changing the subject. Two of the statuettes were shaped like loaves of bread, with an unattractive brown glaze, the third a fish in moulded and unfired clay.

"Somehow, I doubt you will."

The buzzer sounded, alien in the calm space.

"Erin, it's Pete. Coming up."

Anne offered coffee to Pete and drifted into the kitchen area while he talked to Erin. Their voices were low but carried to where she was working.

"What did the guy look like?"

"Five eleven or six feet, dark hair, black eyes, a long nose, high cheekbones. I don't know about his teeth. He didn't smile. Aggressive. As I said, the woman wandered around, and I had to keep an eye on her. Distracting the shopkeeper while someone steals is an old trick. When he noticed that I was watching her, he said something in what I took to be Russian, and she came and stood beside him."

"You said they were aggressive?"

"Yes. They wanted an instant appraisal, and they wanted the jewels back. That doesn't happen, especially with old jewels because it's not only the intrinsic value, but also the value as an antique, and they claimed these were Romanov pieces. I insisted that I would send them and the report to the lawyer."

"Where are they?"

"Here in the safe."

Erin unlocked it, took out three cases covered in deep blue velvet, and opened them.

"So beautiful," Anne said.

One jewel was a simple stem of diamonds, with an emerald flower surrounded by more diamonds, another a hatpin set with a natural pearl with two diamonds, and the last a natural pearl, encircled by diamonds, and suspended beneath it, another teardrop pearl, surmounted with diamonds.

"What value, Erin?"

"Together, very close to one hundred thousand dollars, if not more."

"This one," Anne said, pointing to the two-pearl jewel.

"Yes."

"What?" asked Pete.

"The pearl is the most valuable. But all have the Fabergé mark so that auction value could be higher."

Erin folded the jewels in their protective velvet cloths, closed the cases, and returned them to the safe.

"I have to ask you some questions, Erin. First, do you own

a gun?"

"Yes."

Oh no, Anne thought. Now Erin would be on his suspect list. The only one, for now, except for herself.

"Where is it?"

"In my bedside table. I keep it in a safe when Adam is here, but he wants me to keep it in my bedroom when he's away."

"Show me."

Erin led the way but stood aside as Pete opened the drawer and pulled out the weapon. He bagged it.

"Why—"

"For comparison."

"You don't think—"

"I don't think, Erin. I follow procedure and think after I get some facts."

Erin turned to Anne, her brown eyes full of tears. Anne put her arm around Erin, took out her phone and sent a text to Thomas. *Two minutes,* he replied. Two minutes.

Pete left.

"What can I do?" she said. "What can I do? He thinks I killed that woman."

"No, he doesn't, but he doesn't want anyone to say he ignored you. Call Adam. In the meantime, Thomas is coming."

Guns, Anne thought. Again, guns and killing. She trembled at a memory of the assassin's dead eyes staring into hers. Someone was shaking her and calling her name.

"Anne? What happened?"

"A memory, only a memory."

The doorbell rang, and Erin went to answer. Thomas was there.

Ivan swung his car into the parking space below his unit and ran up the stairs. Inside, he collapsed into the one chair and wept. He'd find her, he thought. He'd find her and kill her, but first, he would take the egg. He wiped his face with his hands and rummaged through Dasha's suitcase, flinging her clothes on the bed. Now and then he paused, to smell her scent and sob. Under her nightgown, wrapped in a silk scarf—her favourite, the green one with elephants and tigers—he found their wedding picture. He kissed her photo, bundled it in the scarf, and stowed it between his shirts. He checked his computer. An email from Colette.

Where are you?

He roared, swearing at Colette, and grasped the computer. The words mocked him. He smashed the laptop on the desk until the hated words disappeared. He would kill her, but first, he wanted the egg. He took his gun from its hiding place inside the suitcase, shoved it in his pocket, and left the room, abandoning the rest.

The motel office was dark. He'd paid three days in advance, and no one cared in this place if he stayed or went. Inside the car, he gripped the wheel with white-knuckled fingers. He'd go north, find a place to hide and decide how to get the egg from that stupid girl in the shop, and he'd kill Colette. He'd make her suffer and kill her, slow.

An hour later, he stopped for gas. When he went inside to pay, he noticed a card at the register advertising cabins for rent. He took a picture with his phone and drove north again, this time to the address in the advertisement.

Dawn broke over the mountains by the time he pulled into the lane beside the mailbox. Ahead, he saw lights downstairs in a house. Good, he thought. Farm people, up early.

A curious dog rounded the corner of the building when he parked and barked a warning. A German Shepherd ambled toward the car from the other direction and sat, waiting. He tapped on the horn. A few moments later, a lanky, older man, with a grizzled beard and holding a coffee cup, opened the door.

"Come in," the man said.

Ivan followed him into the kitchen where a scrubbed pine table was set for two. At the stove, a young woman, not much older than seventeen or so, fried bacon in a black, cast-iron pan on a wood stove reminding Ivan he was hungry. The man waved Ivan to a chair at the table.

"Coffee?" he said.

"Thanks."

He put a mug in front of Ivan and pushed the sugar and cream towards him. After a few moments of silence, while they both drank, the man said, "Do something for you this morning?"

"You have cabins for rent in the mountains?"

"Yup. Five hundred the week. In advance."

"I will not need a week."

"Only way I rent."

Ivan looked over at the girl. Pretty. Brown hair and freckles over one of those little American noses. She dumped the bacon on a paper-covered plate and put it in an oven in the wood stove.

"Credit cards?"

"Nope."

"Call off the dogs. My money's in the van."

"Yep."

Minutes later, map in hand, Ivan left. Now he had a place to bring the woman from the antique store. She would tell him what he wanted to know.

~

Back in the farmhouse, Maddy served bacon and eggs to her grandfather, Will.

"I don't think you should have rented to him, Grandpa. He looked mean."

"Russky, I think. They all look mean."

Chapter Seven

Thomas drove the few minutes into town in a worried state of mind. How would Anne withstand yet another dead body, yet another investigation, after her experiences in Bermuda and Spain? Those were on him. He had introduced her to Ari, the Mossad agent who saved her life in Bermuda. Daniel, she called him now, after running with him across Spain and France with the Israeli child. And then, she killed Esti. Her image of herself as a peaceful person died that day, too, and that brought on the nightmares.

He parked on the street and walked past the cruisers lined up behind the building, waving a hand at Pete. He rang the bell and Erin told him to come up.

When Erin let him in, Thomas hugged her and sat beside Anne on the sofa. His dark eyes searched hers.

"Another body, Thomas. Another. Why can't I escape them?"

She turned her face into the rough fabric of his canvas coat for a moment, taking strength from his embrace. She straightened her back.

"I went for a walk this morning and looked in the shop window, Erin's window. At the back, I could see a shape on the floor and that the outside door was open. I ran around the building, and when I came inside, I saw that a woman's body on the floor. I checked, but she was gone. Cold and gone. I called 911, and Pete Graham came. He stayed until a few minutes ago and he took away Erin's pistol."

Thomas glanced across at Erin and saw the fear in her lovely eyes.

"It's routine, Erin. He has to follow it. Have you called Adam?
She nodded her head.

"He's coming from Burlington. An hour or so, he said."

"Tell me about the dead woman."

Anne told him what little they knew, including the Fabergé jewels.

"It sounds like an Agatha Christie novel," he said.

Outside, the distinctive siren of the ambulance sounded as it left the parking lot.

"Why a siren?" Anne asked. "The patient is dead."

A few moments later, Pete spoke to Erin at the door.

"Please keep the shop closed for today, at least. I've left the tape up."

"All right. Can I clean?"

"No, not today. But you can go through. Anything out of place or something that shouldn't be there, you let me know. Did you call Adam?"

"Yes."

"I'll need to speak to him."

He looked past Erin, caught Thomas's eye and nodded to him. Thomas walked over and shook his hand and asked how the new job was.

"Pretty good, although we don't have much serious crime here, except when—"

Thomas cut him off before he could complete what he mentioned Anne's previous discoveries.

"First homicide?"

"Yeah. What are you doing here, Tom?"

"Anne called me. We're together now."

"Didn't know that. You out at your mother's?"

Thomas nodded, and Pete said he might need to talk to Anne or Erin later.

"I'll walk down with you," Thomas said.

～

His feet apart, his right hand resting on his belt, his Stetson in his left, Pete waited for Thomas. He wasn't much taller than Thomas's 5' 9", but stocky where Thomas was lithe. His fair hair was cut short in the military style he still preferred.

"I'm going to take Anne back to Catherine's. I'll take Erin too, if she'll come with me. Any problems with that?" Thomas asked.

"Nope. So long as they're around when I need to talk to them."

"Did you call Adam?"

"Nope. No need."

"He might appreciate a call."

"He's a civilian."

Thomas raised his eyebrows at that.

"Not for long."

Pete stepped back, and his shoulders stiffened.

"What? He's coming back?"

"Not here. Relax. But I heard FBI."

"Don't want to seem to favour nobody."

"Don't bend so far back you fall on your ass. I'm going back up."

When Thomas left him, Pete clicked in the number for Adam's cell. In a moment, he picked up.

"Yeah, Pete."

"Erin call you?"

"Yeah. I'm on my way."

Pete walked towards the back of the shop and watched the medical examiner load the corpse into the van. His deputy, his brother Dave, loped across the parking lot towards him but stopped when Pete put up a hand.

"What's that supposed to mean?"

"Thought you should know."

"Now I do. Where's Erin?"

"Upstairs."

"She'll be there."

Not a question, Pete thought. A command. He'd let it go. Adam's voice had that iron edge to it that meant *don't push me.*

"Yeah."

Pete turned towards his brother and waved him on.

"Id?"

"Not yet."

"Nobody saw nothing, Pete. Too early, I guess," Dave said.

"Yeah."

He drove back to the station.

~

Erin sat on the edge of her chair and leaned forward toward Anne. She looked young and vulnerable with no makeup, her hair caught up by a scarlet band, her dark green sweatshirt from college proclaiming support for the University of Vermont Catamounts. Her long fingers, captured on her lap, writhed and twisted.

"What am I going to do? He thinks I killed her."

Anne reached forward and stilled Erin's hands.

"Try to relax, Erin. You haven't done anything. He'll test your gun, and then he'll turn you back into a witness."

Erin's brown eyes glistened with unspilled tears.

"Will you take the jewels and the statuettes? I don't want them here in case they come back."

"Perhaps Pete—"

Erin shook her head, and her jaw tightened.

"He didn't ask for them, and they aren't mine. I don't want them to go into some police lock-up for years."

"He may want them back when he realizes he didn't bag them."

"I'll say I sent them away for safe-keeping."

"If that's what you want, but I think you should talk to Adam about them."

"I will."

Erin took two velvet-covered jewel cases from the safe, put them and the statuettes in a bag, and handed it to Anne.

"Are you coming back with me?"

"No, Adam is coming."

Downstairs, Thomas waited for her, his dark eyes full of concern. He put his arms around her, and she sheltered there for a moment.

"I'll take you back to Catherine's if you want. Is Erin coming?" he said.

"No. She said she'd wait for Adam."

"Won't you come back out with me?"

"Not tonight. I want you to talk to your family and make sure I'm welcome, before I come out again. And I want to put Erin's jewels in Catherine's safe."

"Someone dangerous wants those jewels."

"But whoever it is, doesn't know who I am or that I have them. I'll be fine. I'm worried about Erin though. You said Adam talked to Pete?"

"Yes, he's on his way."

Anne slid into the front seat of the car beside him, the purse on her lap heavy with jewels, her mind burdened with fear.

Thomas turned the key in the SUV, the vehicle that he used when he garaged his favourite Honda Prelude for the winter. He reached for Anne, his lips brushing hers, put the car in gear and drove away from the square, around the block to the street that led to Catherine's.

"How are you?" he asked.

He glanced towards her and back at the snow-covered street.

"I don't know. I walked this morning because I had another nightmare about Esti. I think I'll never get over this. Whatever this is?"

She kept her eyes forward, her face pale and immobile. She tried so hard to maintain control, to keep her fears to herself.

"PTSD."

"It feels wrong to say that. I haven't been in combat; I haven't seen the horrible things the soldiers have; I haven't done the things they've done."

"What you've been through is bad enough for a gentle paediatrician from a gentle country."

He stopped the car by the pond. She needed to talk. He needed to talk to her.

"Should I go home. Would it be easier for you with the girls?" she said.

"The girls and I talked. They're sorry, and they recognize now that Mom is ill."

The girls, especially Cecee, weren't all that reasonable but they would behave in his house, towards the woman he loved or they would leave. But that wouldn't work. He couldn't send his children away, and Anne wouldn't let that happen.

"You should take her to a neurologist."

"She's adamant that she doesn't want medical care. I don't want to upset her so close to Christmas. Maybe after. What difference will a few days make if she has Alzheimer's?"

"If that's what's wrong. We can't be sure until she's had an evaluation. There are treatable—"

"No. After Christmas."

Dammit, why was he so abrupt? Her face changed, closed up. No talking now.

"Up to you," she said. "We should go back to Catherine's."

"And then I'll go back to the house."

Back at the loft, the sound of the key in the lock brought Erin across the room and into Adam's arms, when he stepped through the doorway. Now, she thought. Now she was safe. She looked up into

Adam's brown eyes, traced the curve of his nose, broken in some long-ago football game and patted his cheek.

"I'm okay," she said. "Now, I'm okay."

"What the hell did Pete think he was doing, treating you like a suspect?"

He prowled the room, stopped at the window to check the square, came back to Erin and wrapped his arms around her.

"He has to do his job."

Adam snorted.

"There's more than one way to do a job. He knows you and what you are to me."

"He's new, and this is his first—"

"He was my deputy for years. He's been a cop for years. He should know."

Erin walked to the kitchen and plugged in the kettle.

"He took your gun?" Adam said to her back.

"Yes."

"I should get it back before I leave."

"No. I don't want it. I wouldn't be able to use it. Not after seeing that woman's body."

She added three bags of her favourite Lady Grey tea and water.

"I forgot to warm the pot."

Her eyes filled with tears and she covered her face and sobbed.

Adam came to her and put his arms around her.

"What if whoever shot her comes back?" he said.

Erin straightened up and wiped her face on a handy dishtowel.

"Why would he come back after killing her?"

"If he killed her."

"You think there's a third person."

"I'm saying we don't know. You should come back to Burlington with me."

She shrugged out of his arms.

"I have to carry in the tea."

"It's not safe here."

"I don't want to be driven away from my home and the store. I armed the security."

"But they bypassed it to get in the store."

She edged past him through the door and set the tray on the square, upholstered ottoman that served as a coffee table.

"Or I was careless. I called the security company, and they are coming to install a better system."

"Come with me until they do."

"No, I want to stay and put the store right again."

She picked up the teapot and set it down again when her shaking hand threatened to drop it. Adam poured, and she stirred sugar into her cup.

"Has Pete finished?"

"He said so. I don't like it, your staying here."

"I'll keep the security on and my phone with me. It will be okay."

"I'll call Pete to see if he'll have someone outside, for tonight."

"Okay. If I get scared, I'll go to Catherine's."

An hour later, Adam left for Burlington and Erin went downstairs to clean the shop.

Chapter Eight

After Adam left, Erin went down to her shop and walked through. What a mess the scene-of-the-crime crew had made. Pete told her not to clean up but to check again for anything moved or missing. Her lovely shop, covered with fingerprint powder and that awful stain on the floorboards. When Pete said she could clean, she would do it herself. Too many fragile pieces to leave it to others.

The chimes over the front door sounded, and she jumped, rocking the glass and steel table beside her. Her chest tightened, and fear froze her in place, but then she steadied the table and turned towards the door. She hadn't put on the alarm while she waited for a delivery from her picker, who'd promised some treasures from a barn somewhere in New Hampshire, and for the serviceman from the security firm. A dark figure stood against the light from the front windows. In a moment, Erin knew him.

She vaulted to her feet and ran towards the back door. He thundered after her. Before she unlocked the door, he was on her, his arm around her throat. The rough fabric of his jacket rasped against her skin, releasing the pungency of years of smoking mixed with cheap cologne. She gasped and stopped struggling before she would lose consciousness.

"That's a good girl. Now turn the lock."

"What do—"

"Shut up. Do you have money?"

"In my purse."

"Where is it?"

"Desk."

He dragged her down the room, grabbed her purse, and thrust it into her arms. The door opened out, and he pushed her through ahead of him and towards a white box van parked opposite. Her knees hit the running board, pain shot up her legs, and she groaned.

"Shut up."

His arms closed around her and heaved her onto the floor of the van. The smell of stale coffee and staler sweat gagged her.

"What do—"

He slapped her, not enough to hurt, but enough to remind her to be quiet. Ivan something. He came with the woman, the dead woman. Did he kill her? What did he want with her? She concentrated on his face. His black eyes, expressionless over Slavic cheekbones and a hawked nose, avoided hers. He'd let her see him. Why? Was he going to kill her? He had a hard mouth. A hard man.

He wound duct tape around her wrists and ankles and spread a piece across her mouth. She liked duct tape, liked its usefulness, but now...

She concentrated on breathing, in and out through a nose stuffy from the smells in the truck. She couldn't breathe. Her heart raced, and she thought she would die, here in the back of this filthy van. Panic. Breathe. In and out. In and out. Her heart slowed.

He slammed the door of the van and moments later the engine turned over, the van accelerated, and it was all she could do to stay upright. She braced her legs against the side. Where was he taking her? What did he want? If it were the jewels, why didn't he force her to take him to them? But he hadn't mentioned the jewels. Perhaps he was one of those serial... No, she wouldn't think that, wouldn't go there. Not yet.

Adam. What would he do? Then, she wept.

Chapter Nine

E arlier that day, Colette chose a table in the window overlooking the parking lot rather than the expansive back garden of the B&B. She nibbled at a croissant and sipped excellent cafe au lait while she planned.

Today, she would check out of this place and drive to Burlington to a hotel, not too close to the centre of town, with quick access to the interstate, and large enough to guarantee some anonymity. But no one was looking for her. Ivan was the focus of the police attention, she was sure.

Someone passed by, a little too close to her table. A jolt of panic hit her stomach; she held her breath and slipped her right hand into her purse. The man—tall, black, good-looking, confident—strode to the breakfast bar, picked up his choices and coffee and sat across the room with his back to her. She breathed again and picked up her knife to add jam to her pastry. Not interested in her.

Later, she drove along the interstate, stuck for long kilometres behind a snowplough, watching her rear-view mirror for any signs of a pursuer.

The hotel, a grey clapboard low-rise, green roofs shining in the morning sunshine, squatted on a street, close to the off-ramp. Colette drove through the portico, left her luggage, and parked in the large lot beyond. The doors opened to a lobby made cheerful by wooden accents and a stone fireplace.

She had booked an upgrade, with a larger room and the option of a lounge reserved for those who paid the extra fee. But she hadn't considered pumpkin-coloured walls and plaid drapes. She opened them to a view of the Green Mountains on the horizon. Mountains. Perhaps she would drive there, into a landscape that might remind her of her Swiss home.

The linen, however, was all white and the bed comfortable. Colette hung her clothes in the closet and opened a unit she travelled with that let her avoid putting her clothes in suspect drawers. That done, she texted Ivan.

Where are you?

I have the woman.

No. What have you done? We were supposed to run a quiet operation.

You were. I want the egg and I will kill you.

Which woman?

The one from the shop.

Fool. You will not find me so easy to kill.

Ivan would try to kill her. He would want his revenge as she wanted hers on McPhail. She would have to tell Alexei, and he was far more dangerous than Ivan.

She tapped in the numbers on the satellite phone that Alexei had given her.

"Da."

"The fool has kidnapped the owner of the antique store," she said.

"You are unable to control your people or yourself."

"He is not "my people". You forced him and his maniac wife on me, and now she is dead, and he is going to kill an American, an American whose fiancé is a cop."

"A cop?"

"He was. Now he is a law student until he joins the FBI or some other government police. Yes, and he won't stop until he finds me and then you."

"He won't find me unless you—"

"I will focus on the egg and McPhail."

"Forget McPhail, get the egg and—"

"No."

She hung up on him. She had never done that. What would he do? What could he do, from Russia? She felt a shudder of fear. Because he used a satellite phone didn't mean he was in Russia. He could be in the next room.

She threw the phone on the bed but a moment later retrieved it and tucked it into her purse. The room wasn't secure. No room in this country was secure.

What should she do? Try to find Ivan and rescue the woman and take the egg from her? At least, she would follow McPhail.

She had to go out to shop for clothes that didn't mark her as European. People noticed her as she dressed now and would remember her. She would shop and then she would find McPhail.

∼

Adam wheeled his truck along the highway, its shoulders blurred by heavy snow that thickened on the windshield, slowing the wipers. He peered forward, happy to see the lights that marked the outskirts of the city.

When he reached his apartment near the University, he parked in the underground and rode the elevator to the third floor. Inside, he clicked the number on his cell that called Erin. Straight to message. That was odd. She worried and usually kept it on when he was driving back. She'd call him, likely as soon as she got off the phone. But when he came out of the shower, she hadn't called.

Where was she? He prowled the small spacet. The apartment wasn't home. A place to eat in, sleep in. A place without Erin. She tried to make it comfortable, bringing furniture from the shop, pieces he could stretch out on, like the worn, brown leather sofa. He'd told her he didn't want it re-upholstered. A picture from Bermuda stood on the table in the corner where he studied. The two of them, arms around each other, on the Railway Trail where he proposed. She brought other objects from the shop—pillows, one of those a bright scarlet, a blanket in navy with red stripes, a set of three vases, Navajo, she said. None of it mattered. The only thing he wanted from the shop was her.

He wolfed a sandwich, watching the snow filter down onto the cars in the outside lot, turning them into strange northern animals. He had an exam in three weeks, but he couldn't settle. He turned on the television, watched CNN for a while, calling Erin every half-hour. When two hours had passed since he got in, he called Pete.

"Pete Graham."

"Adam. Have you got Erin down at the station?"

He could hear the anger in his own voice.

"No. Why?"

"I can't reach her."

"Didn't she go back with you?"

"No. The gun?"

"Clean. Maybe trouble with her phone. Lots of wires down."

"Can you have someone swing by?"

"Yup."

"Call me back."

Again, he watched the talking heads on the news programmes discussing the latest tweets from Washington, not caring, waiting. The cars below had disappeared under their blankets of snow. One man, wielding a push broom, cleared his, leaving mounds of white surrounding an empty spot when he drove off. Thirty minutes. How long did it take to walk across the square?

The phone buzzed. He picked it up before the second sound.

"Did—"

"Her place is dark, locked tight; the apartment too. Out with friends?"

Pete didn't sound worried but a little nervous talking to his old boss. He likely thought he was over-reacting.

"She didn't say she was going out."

"Might turn the phone off in a restaurant?"

"She always does. It's a thing with her."

"We'll check later."

"No, now".

No answer. Pete hadn't heard him, he thought. He wasn't chippy, didn't take offence, but how would he respond to Adam giving orders? Would he search for her? He slumped on the cold leather of the sofa and waited.

∿

In Culver's Mills, Pete noted the dark windows of Erin's shop and the apartment above. He'd swing by Catherine's. Adam was pissed and if he knew him, and he did, he'd be back in Culver's within the hour, unless he located Erin in the next few minutes.

No lights on at Catherine's. Where the hell was every woman in town? He knew Anne liked Evan's restaurant. At the door, he asked for Mary, the owner.

"I'm sorry, but they're in France," said the hostess who doubled as the concierge for the rooms upstairs.

"I'm looking for Erin Maxwell."

"I'm sorry, but I'm new and—"

"Do you know Catherine LaPlante or Anne McPhail."

"The doctor who finds bodies. Yes. She hasn't been here tonight."

Damn woman. Where else would she go?

He slogged down the street to Lil's Diner. The door at the top of the stairs opened to the sounds of quiet conversation. No kids this time of night, Pete thought. Peg served behind the counter.

"Have you seen Erin Maxwell or Catherine LaPlante this evening?"

"Yes, Catherine and Anne McPhail were in earlier but left about ten minutes ago. I haven't seen Erin today. I imagine she is too upset to be out and about."

"I need to find her. If you see her, will you ask her to call me?"

"Sure. Why—"

"Thanks."

He sat in the cruiser, going over what he knew about Erin and then remembered that she belonged to the little theatre group, but when he called, the director told him they didn't have a rehearsal that night, and he hadn't seen Erin.

He left his car and walked the streets towards Catherine's. The snow fell more heavily now, shrouding the buildings and creating halos around the street lights. He frightened Erin by demanding her gun and treating her like a suspect. At the weir, the river flowed dark and the pond above, partly covered with ice, betrayed no evidence of a jumper. He walked on, guilt tracking his steps.

Further along, he saw the two women ahead of him, ploughing through the drifts. His approach silenced by the snow, he was at their backs before they heard him. Anne swung around, her keys in her hand. Worried and scared, he guessed. Silver-grey fur around the hood of her blue parka framed her small face. Melting snow trickled down her forehead. She dropped the keys in her pocket and held out a hand.

"Pete. You scared me."

"Sorry. I'm trying to find Erin. Do you know where she is?"

The two women looked at each other and shook their heads in unison.

"No, not since this morning," Anne said.

"I didn't see her today at all," Catherine said, "but Anne told me she was distraught."

"Yeah, I know. Some of that's on me. I called the little theatre guy and went to Evan's, and Lil's. Anywhere else?"

"She might be in church. She goes to the Auld Kirk," Catherine said.

"I'll try over there."

At the church, the pastor told him Erin didn't attend the service that evening.

With nowhere left to look, Pete put out a bulletin about her when he got back to the office. He reached for the phone, but paused for a moment, going over his search, making sure he hadn't forgotten anything or anywhere, before he called Adam.

"No sign of her, Adam."

"I'm on my way."

"I'll meet you at her shop."

This was a meeting he wasn't looking forward to. Adam's temper was slow but where Erin was concerned...

~

In Burlington, Adam paced again, fighting against the impulse to get back in the truck and drive to Culver's. Maybe Tom Beauchamp took them out to dinner. He scrolled through his contacts until he found the number.

"Tom? Adam."

"What's up."

"Do you know where Anne and Catherine and Erin are? Are they together?"

"No idea. Why?"

Why didn't he know where Anne was? They were supposed to be together. He controlled his anger and told Thomas what was up.

"I can't find Erin. She's not answering her phone. Pete went by and the shop's dark."

"Did you call Anne?"

"I don't have—"

"I'll do it and call back."

A few moments later, the phone buzzed again.

"No answer. She's either still upset and not talking to me, or has it turned off for dinner."

"Why... No, don't bother to tell me."

"I'll find them."

Thomas's confident voice disappeared and left Adam staring out his window again. He swore, thumped the window sill with his fist, threw on his coat, and raced down to his truck. In a few minutes, he hit the snow-covered, empty highway. Why didn't Pete call?

Why didn't he insist that Erin come with him? She was so stubborn. Someone, someone she knew, someone who knew her, killed that woman. What would he do if he had her? He focussed on the road, burying the dread. A few miles more and he would find her. His phone rang.

~

Adam swung into the parking lot behind Erin's shop, beside Pete's truck.

"Have you been inside?" he asked when Pete swung out of his truck and walked with him to the loading door.

"No. Waited for you. Key?"

"Yeah."

But security wasn't on and the door was unlocked.

"You didn't check the back door?" he asked.

"No, I went on to Catherine's, when there was no answer from upstairs."

He hesitated before pushing the door open. What if she were there, another broken body, abandoned on the floor of the shop? He forced his stricken lungs to breathe and went in. He flicked the switch in the darkened store. Two lamps, one a Tiffany-shaded brass candlestick and the other an art-deco lady with a pink shade, glowed in the room settings that Erin set up to feature her antiques. No body, but an overturned table blocked the way down the central aisle.

"A struggle?" Pete said.

"Yeah. She wouldn't leave it like this."

His cell phone vibrated its urgent message.

"What is it?" Pete said.

"A text. Someone says he has Erin and wants the egg. What egg?"

"Ask him."

Adam texted back asking *what egg?*

The reply was swift. *Like you don't know. 72 hours. No cops.*

"What the—"

Adam dropped into a chair, reading the words on the phone. Seventy-two hours. Seventy-two hours or what? Pete took the phone from Adam's white-knuckled fingers, read the text and called his office. He gave precise instruction to Dave, his brother and deputy, and squatted beside Adam.

"Come on, man. We have to look around. The SOC guys will be here but try to find something about the goddam jewels or egg. Whatever that is?

Adam shrugged out of his parka, threw it behind him, turned on the overhead lights and rummaged in Erin's desk, searching for the letter from the law firm that employed her. After thumbing through bills and orders, he turned to her file cabinet that stood in the gloom at the back of the office. Pete toured the shop, checked the front door, and stood, watching.

Locked, of course, Adam thought. Why did she lock the file cabinet and not put on the alarm? He shook his head. No use asking why. He recovered the key to the file drawer from the pen tray on the desk and opened it. Filed by what? Date, person, object. A few minutes perusal showed him that she filed by object. Under a tab labelled jewellery, he found sub-headings, one of which was a gemnology request. The letter, from a law firm, Hunter and Todd of Burlington, detailed the contents of the assignment. He called Anne and put her on speaker for Pete to listen.

"Anne? Adam. You're on speaker; Pete is here with me at the shop. What jewels did Erin give you to hold for her?"

"Two brooches, one with a single large pearl and one with emeralds. Also, a ring set with a garnet and diamonds and another with sapphires."

"No egg."

"Not unless he's calling the pearl an egg."

"Could be it. Thanks, Anne."

Adam wrote a list of the jewels in the small notebook he'd carried since he became a police officer. He'd need a new one soon.

"Why would he call it an egg when it's a pearl. I think it's a stretch," Pete said. "I should have taken them with me when she showed them to me."

"This letter doesn't say whose property they are. Erin wouldn't have considered them her property, and she wouldn't have let you take them without a warrant. She takes her fiduciary duty seriously."

Adam drummed his fingers on the letter, folded it, and refiled it.

"'Do you think the law firm would tell you?"

"Maybe. I know Frank Hunter, the senior partner."

"From law school?"

"No, from a case here."

"Can we look at the safe?"

"Nothing there, but sure."

Upstairs, Adam prowled the apartment, looking for anything else that might hint what the egg was, but found nothing. The SOC team arrived, and Pete went down to talk to them. Adam ran the names on his phone until he found Frank Hunter's home number.

The lawyer's voice, still young and vibrant, in spite of his age, growled into the phone, "I hope you've got a good reason for interrupting dinner with my grandchildren, Lieutenant Davidson."

"Yes, sir. But I'm a law student now, not a cop."

"Then why—"

"My fiancée's been kidnapped."

"I'm sorry, but what—"

"The kidnapper seems to want something in the collection that you sent to her. She's Erin Maxwell, a gemologist and antique dealer in Culvers."

"Has the collection been stolen?"

"No. He wants something he's calling an egg. Perhaps the largest pearl. Perhaps something else. Who do they belong to?"

"I can't tell you that."

Adam gripped the phone, willed his voice to lose the edge he knew it had.

"It's pertinent to the investigation of a kidnapping, sir. Wouldn't your client want to help?"

"She lives in Shady Gables retirement home, just outside Culver's. I chose Ms. Maxwell because the owner had read about her. I'll ask if I can reveal her name to you."

"Tonight? We have less than seventy-two hours."

"Very well. I'll call you back."

When the phone rang, Adam took down the name of the client.

"She said not tonight, Adam. She's not a well woman."

"But—"

"Not tonight."

Adam slumped in the chair Erin kept for him through all the furniture swapping. Anne. She'd come with him and help him with the lady at the nursing home. Nothing to do now, except wait for morning, but he had to do something. Ten minutes later he knocked on Catherine's door.

Chapter Ten

Snow shrouded the street lamps and blurred the Christmas lights that decorated the houses along the street towards Catherine's. Thomas peered ahead. Two figures trudged head-down through the falling snow, arm in arm, supporting each other when one or the other slipped on the ice-y sidewalk. He pulled ahead of the two women and parked. He waited until they drew closer, opened the door when they reached him and climbed out. One of them, in a dark wool coat and furry white hat, called to him.

"Thomas. What are you doing in town?" Anne said.

She waited for him at the gate in the fence that surrounded the B&B.

"I'll go ahead," said Catherine and walked up the steps to the porch and in the house.

"Pete called to say Erin was missing. I came in to stay with you and Catherine until we know what's going on."

"You think something's happened to her?"

"Pete can't find her."

Anne clutched his arm. She had surprising strength in her small hand. He patted it and tucked her arm into the crook of his.

"We spoke to him a few minutes ago. He went to the church to—"

"Come inside," Catherine called from the open door.

She hung their coats on hooks by the front door and brought tea to her front parlour, a long room lined with bookshelves, a brick fireplace with a pine mantel opposite club chairs big enough for a tall man to sprawl in, and a sofa upholstered in soft green corduroy. A bay window curtained in a muted plaid of green and burgundy overlooked the street.

"What is it, Tom?" Catherine said.

"Erin is missing."

"What do you mean, missing? Pete is still looking, but he hasn't found her yet. We told him to try at the church."

"I spoke to Adam, maybe before Pete went to the church. He'll be on his way back. I want to talk to you about the break-in. I think that whatever they wanted, they didn't find, so they'll be back."

Catherine went to the kitchen. Knowing her, the kettle was going on, and tea would be coming out.

"The jewels," Anne said.

"Yes."

"You should give them to Pete."

"No, Erin wanted me to keep them. They aren't hers. She was evaluating a law firm, and she doesn't want them in some evidence locker somewhere."

She had that look he knew well, the one that said she wouldn't do whatever it was.

"Pete will get a warrant."

"Not if he doesn't know they're here. Not if we don't tell him."

A flicker of a smile crossed his face.

"You've been spending too much time with Mossad."

Catherine carried in a tray, laden with teapot and cups, sugar and milk and cookies and set it on a side table.

"What next?" Catherine said. "What will they do next to find her."

The doorbell rang, and someone pounded on the door.

"Police," Thomas said.

~

Thomas came back with Adam, his face grey and stricken.

Catherine poured a tumbler of Bourbon and handed to Adam. He drank half, closed his eyes, and leaned back in the chair, his cheeks flushed from the alcohol.

"What's happened?" Anne said, going to him.

"Erin's been kidnapped."

No, she thought. Not that Russian.

"How—"

"He sent a text."

Anne sat beside him on the sofa and put her arm around him. Her eyes met Thomas's.

"What does he want? Money?" Thomas said. "I can—"

"No, he wants the egg, whatever in hell that is. But thanks, Tom."

Could it be a Fabergé egg, Anne wondered. There was no Fabergé egg in the collection of jewels. Hopeless.

Catherine walked out of the room and up the stairs. When she returned, she had a suitcase with her and her coat on.

"Catherine?" Adam said.

"I'm sorry, but I have to go in a few moments. I'm going to Toronto to spend the holidays with my family, and the limo to the airport is outside."

Anne gave her a quick hug

"I'd forgotten. Have a lovely time with your family," she said.

"Please stay here as long as you like."

The doorbell rang, Catherine waved and was gone.

Thomas's worried gaze met hers, but before they could talk, the doorbell rang. Pete stood on the doorstep.

"Adam here?"

"Yeah."

Adam came out and spoke to Pete at the door.

"I'm going down to the station with Pete."

"Call later if you want, Adam."

"I will."

The room emptied, and Anne and Thomas were left, standing apart in the silence. Should she go with him? Could she stay here alone? Maggie, Catherine's dog, was spending Christmas at a farm. She gave herself a mental shake. She had been in a worse situation, alone with a child who needed protection.

"Now will you stay with me?" said Thomas, mirroring her thoughts.

"Not until I see for myself how things are with your family."

"Are you sure?"

"Yes. Why would the kidnapper come here? He has Erin, and he thinks Adam will get him the egg."

"Then," he said, "I'll stay too."

"What about your family?"

"What about them? I don't seek permission every time I stay away from home, but I'll call and let them know what's going on."

"Dinner?"

"Evan's?"

"No. I'll check the kitchen."

While Thomas phoned his family, she put water on to boil for pasta and made a quick tomato, onion, and black olive sauce. She was grating Parmesan when he walked in. She glanced from her pan to his face.

"It didn't go well?"

"Cecilia, not Daniel. I'll talk to all of them about their attitude."

"But what is it? Do they dislike me that much? Why?"

"Only Cecilia and I think she's terrified about her grandmother. She clung to her after my wife died and she's always been closer than the other two."

"The others have families of their own, and she has only you two. Are you going back out?"

"No. I'll go back in the morning, but tonight, I want to be alone with you. It's been a long time since Spain."

Chapter Eleven

Erin braced against the side-wall of the van, but swayed towards the back. They were climbing, she thought. He was taking her to the mountains. They slowed, made a turn, and climbed again. She rubbed her face against the wall, trying to pull the duct tape away from her nose. It gave a little, enough so that her nose was clear and breathing easier.

How long had it been? Hours, perhaps? It couldn't be hours. They'd be at the border if they were going north, into the Green Mountains. Or they could be going east, towards New Hampshire and the White Mountains. The vehicle skidded, and her head hit the wall. Pain shot across her head and down her back. Warm liquid trickled across her face. Blood. She tried to focus, but her eyes blurred and she drifted away. Before she lost consciousness, the door opened, and Ivan was there.

"Get out."

She tried to form the words that would say she couldn't but fell forward. Ivan grabbed her and hauled her out of the vehicle.

"What's this blood?"

"Hit head when the van crashed."

"We didn't crash. A skid only. Come on."

Erin struggled to stand, her legs dull and heavy.

"Can't walk."

"Yes, you can."

He dragged her through the snow, supporting her weight on his arm, towards a mountain cabin. Her hands numbed in the cold and snow spilled into her shoes. He hauled her up to the porch and leaned her against the wall while he fumbled with a key. Inside, he sat her in a chair and took the duct tape off her wrists. Pain coursed through them as the blood returned and the colour turned from white to scarlet. She moaned.

"What's wrong with your hands."

"It's a condition, called Renaud's. The cold cuts off the circulation to my hands. I could lose fingers."

Her jeans and old sweatshirt hadn't been much protection against the cold in the back of the van. Now that he'd dragged her through the snow, her feet were freezing too.

"What about now."

"They'll be okay, but I need to take off my wet shoes and warm my feet."

"Do it."

She tore off her old sneakers and soaking socks and rubbed her feet.

"I must dig out the van, so I tie you up again."

"Where would I go?"

"I know you would try to escape or kill me, with a knife."

"I won't—"

"Shut up."

He duct-taped her to the chair and left her.

After a time, she heard the engine rumble and catch. A few minutes later, he came back.

"Do you have your cell phone in your pocket?"

"Why—"

"Answer."

"No."

"I don't believe you. All Americans carry the stupid phones all the time. Where is it?"

"On my desk in my shop."

"You are wearing a ring. Who is the man? I want to contact him."

What did he want with Adam? What should she do? What had he said when they talked about a kidnapping. Always cooperate. Stay alive.

"Adam Davidson."

"What is his number?"

Ivan moved his thumbs over the keyboard of his phone when she told him.

"Now, we shall see how much he loves you."

He tapped in text and waited.

∽

Ivan clumped up and down the room, pausing to bellow at Erin.

"Stupid woman. Where are the jewels? Did you give them to someone? Your friend in the store, did you give them to her?"

"What friend. I told you I don't know the French—"

"Not her. Not that bitch. Your friend that came in the store when Dasha and me were there."

What should she do? Adam said cooperate. But what would he do to Anne? What if he kidnapped her too? What if he killed her? Anne didn't have the egg to give to him.

"Anne. Her name is Anne."

"Where does she live?"

"She doesn't live here. She's staying with her friend Thomas or at Catherine's Bed and Breakfast."

"What is his name?"

He slapped her, sending pain shooting over her scalp. The copper taste of blood filled her mouth. She spat again.

"Thomas Beauchamp. He lives in the stone house with the blue door on the west side of the town. Mallory Road."

"And the woman?"

"Catherine's Bed and Breakfast. I don't know the street."

He prowled again and then stooped to glare into her face. His face, dominated by high cheekbones, contorted with rage. His dark eyes, inches from hers, narrowed. Cold, she thought. For all the anger, he's a cold man. He'd kill her when he got the egg.

"How do I get in?"

"Where?"

"The Beauchamp house."

"I don't know. I don't go there."

He raised his fist to hit her again.

"Don't. No matter how many times you hit me, I can't make it up. I keep a shop; they're wealthy. How would I know how to get in the house?"

"Would this Anne?"

"Yes, no, I don't know. I suppose so. She's visited there. Maybe she's staying out there."

"And this inn where the Catherine lives. How do I get in there?"

She sent a silent apology to Anne and Catherine. Maybe they would not be home. Wasn't Catherine going to Canada? Yes. If Anne went to Thomas's, she would be safe with him.

"At the rear. It backs on a lane that isn't well-travelled. Maybe there."

"Then that is where I shall go. But I am hungry. There is food in the cupboard. Make something."

She got to her feet, stumbled on her first steps, but straightened, and walked to the refrigerator. Eggs, bacon, bread: she carried the packages to the stove and began. She cracked the eggs, ate some of the bacon, hoping he wouldn't hear and swallowed a raw egg. Behind her, his footsteps paced the length of the room and back again, mumbling.

A few moments later, Ivan paced the cabin, shaking the cell phone.

"Your boyfriend is a fool."

"What did he say."

"He asked what egg."

"What are you asking him for? What egg?"

"She died because of that egg. Don't tell me you don't know what egg."

"The woman who died, was she your wife?"

"Yes."

"I didn't kill her."

He stopped in front of her chair.

"I know that. Dasha died before my eyes. The French bitch, she killed her."

"What French woman?"

"She hired us—"

If she let him tell her everything, he would kill her, whatever Adam did.

"No," she shouted. "No. Don't tell me. I don't want to know anything. I don't have your egg. I never had an egg. All I have is the jewellery."

"Tell me where you hid it."

"I never had it."

He walked behind her. Her shoulders tensed and pain shot over her scalp as he pulled back on her hair and stared into her eyes and whispered.

"You lie. Your boyfriend has seventy-two hours. Less."

He let go of her hair and circled her again.

"Where is the egg?"

"I don't know."

His fist hit her jaw, she tasted blood and vomited over her sweater and his shoes. Her tongue found a space where a tooth should have been. Did she swallow it? No. She spat the tooth into her lap.

"What did you do? Blood all over me. Stupid woman."

"Me? You hit me."

"I'll hit you again. Spoil that pretty smile unless you tell me what you did with the egg."

"You'll kill me anyway."

"You'll wish I would kill you before I finish with you."

"Where is it?"

Erin closed her eyes and tumbled sideways to the floor. Dust rose around her, and she coughed.

"What the fuck. What are you doing?"

"I fainted. I need some water."

Ivan picked her up and sat her on an armchair near the sofa. He cut the tape around her legs and pulled it off and freed her hands.

"There is nowhere for you to go. If you don't behave, I tie you again. Okay?"

"Okay."

"Now we wait for your boyfriend's answer. What does he do, your boyfriend?"

"He's a law student."

He looked her up and down. His lips twisted into a sneer.

"A little young for you."

"No, he went back to school."

"What did he do before?"

Should she tell him? What would he do? Would he be scared and kill her? Or would he be scared and not kill her?

"He was a policeman."

"This is who I texted, a cop?"

"Yes."

"Good. Maybe he won't lose his head."

He walked to the sink, filled the basin and dumped in the phone.

"Why—"

"I am not a fool. I know they will try to track the call."

Adam wouldn't lose his head, she thought, but he would be so angry that he would never stop looking for her. Never.

Chapter Twelve

Anne opened her eyes to sunshine streaming in. The smell of coffee mingled with bacon wafted up from the kitchen. Thomas thumped up the stairs and appeared at the door, coffee cup in hand.

"Good morning," he said. "Adam will be here in an hour."

"Thanks," she said, "and thanks for the coffee."

She shrugged herself higher and patted the bed beside her. Thomas sat and handed her the mug.

"How are *we*?" he asked.

"Is that a nurse's *we* as in *how am I*, or are you asking about us?"

"Far too early for word games. About us?"

"We seemed okay last night."

"Anne."

His worried dark eyes met hers. No teasing, Anne thought. Not today.

"Good. We're good but the family—"

"I'll sort that out."

"I don't want a polite, forced acceptance."

"I know. Breakfast in ten minutes."

Ten minutes. She showered, pulled on her jeans and an Arran knit sweater and ran down the stairs.

Later, they sat at the breakfast table and watched the blue jays at the feeder.

"It's almost like home, here," she said. "Same birds, same trees, same snow."

"Almost?"

"This country can never be home to me, Thomas. It's too different in many ways, important ways."

He reached for her hand.

"If we have a home together, it won't be here. I promise."

"Please, don't promise when we don't know about your family."

"I know what I want."

Anne's phone pinged a text from Adam. *Out front.*

"Adam's here. I'll let you know where I am later."

He held her, longer than their usual goodbyes and let her go. Outside, she waved to him where he stood on the porch.

Adam drove up to the takeout window at Tim Horton's, a coffee chain on the highway.

"They're still in business," Anne said. "I wasn't sure the franchise would make a go of things down here."

"Long lineups, too. We're lucky today."

He ordered his double-double and a cappuccino for Anne.

"Where is the retirement home, Adam?"

"Just north of town, on the lake."

"That's a pricey location."

"Yes. I think that's why the lady's selling the jewels. Takes a lot to maintain a person out there."

A few miles later, they drove into a circular driveway that ended at what must have been a single-family mansion in the old days. Broad stone steps led up to a broad porch in front of the white clapboard building. Wings branched off the core of the house at either side. Dark green, working shutters protected the windows on both floors. No accommodating ramp for wheelchairs, Anne thought, but perhaps there was a back entrance for them.

A tall cut-glass vase, holding an arrangement of white lilies, graced one end of the eighteen-century reproduction reception desk. A young woman called the manager for them.

"Mrs. Donsky will be right out."

A tall woman, impeccably-arranged dark brown hair piled high, her long neck draped with an artfully arranged silk scarf, held out graceful fingers to shake Adam's hand and then Anne's.

"You are here to see Mrs. Emily Akers. I believe."

"Yes," Adam said. "Is she well enough?"

"Oh yes. Our guests are well and able to get around, Mr. David-son. If they become disabled, they move to our sister facility in Burlington."

"That must be hard on them," Anne said.

"They know that from the beginning, and make short stays at the home before the final move. It works out quite well."

No nursing home smell here, Anne thought. No bleach with that scent of bodily fluids underneath, even though the perfume from the lilies on the desk did remind her of funeral homes.

The manager led the way to an intimate room, decorated in pink and sunny yellows, that overlooked the garden through French doors on one side and double-hung windows on the other. No lilies, but a simple arrangement of carnations and roses filled the air with fragrance. An elderly woman, her white hair cut short but curly and thick, eyes unclouded still, sat upright in a straight-backed armchair. Dressed for her lunch, Anne thought, in a light blue tweed skirt and sweater, a single strand of pearls around her neck.

"Mrs. Akers, your visitors have arrived."

The alert brown eyes scanned each of them. She'd know them again, Anne thought, as she took the delicate, blue-veined hand in hers.

Mrs. Akers waved her other hand towards the chairs that had been drawn up to hers but held on to Anne's as she sat close to her.

"I believe you want to ask me about my jewellery. My lawyer

was careful not to say why but I assume it has something to do with a crime. I recognize both your names from the newspapers a couple of years ago."

Adam looked at Anne. When she nodded, he said, "My fiancée, Erin Maxwell, has been kidnapped and the kidnapper is demanding the egg from the jewels. Was the big pearl ever called an egg?"

"Not to my knowledge. Do I understand that you plan to give him what he demands?"

"We plan to apprehend him but we have to understand what he wants. I know that the egg, if that is the pearl, is not mine to barter for Erin's life."

The easy tears of old age filled the woman's eyes, and her grip on Anne's hand tightened.

"Tell us about the jewellery," Anne said.

"It is a long story that begins in the Crimea in 1917. My great-grandmother, Galina, was lady's maid to Maria Feodorovna, Dowager Empress of all Russia, the widow of Alexander 111. When the revolution came, Galina fled with her to the Crimea. Maria Feodorovna was there when the reports came that her son Nicholas and all the family were dead. She didn't believe it and never did."

"Never?"

"No."

"What happened next," Anne said.

"Things became worse, and they had to flee to England. She was the sister of the Dowager Queen Alexandra of England and her son, George V, sent the Royal Navy to get her."

"And Galina?"

"Yes. She stayed with the Empress, although many left. Years later, Maria Feodorovna returned to Denmark—you knew she was a Dane?"

Anne nodded.

"But Galina stayed in England. She met a man whom she wanted to marry. The Empress gave her the jewels when she returned to Denmark. The family assumed she was grateful that Galina stayed with her so long. They were Fabergé and valuable now."

"And no one in the family ever sold them."

"No, everyone was proud of Galina and wanted to keep them. But I'm all alone now. I'm the last, and if I don't get the money from the jewels, I'll move to a county home when I become ill."

"You're not sick now," Adam said.

"Yes, my dear, I am. The doctor thinks I may last a year or two."

"And they would send you away?"

"I knew that when I moved here, Anne. It was in the contract."

"Do you know anything about the figurines?"

"Aren't they awful? My grandmother told me her mother loved them, and I was to keep them safe. I'm sure they have no value, but that's what she wanted."

"We'll return everything to you, intact," Adam said.

The old woman's eyes closed for a moment.

"If he wants the pearl, give it to him. Erin has many more years to live."

"Thank you," Adam said. "And now you're not alone. Erin and I will always make sure you are well looked after."

Mrs. Akers shook their hands and reached up a soft cheek for their kisses.

As they drove away, Adam said, "All the same, I don't think the pearl is what this guy wants."

"Neither do I," said Anne. "Do you know about the Faberge Easter eggs?"

"We took something about the missing ones in a course on art fraud. Weren't they made for the Czar?"

"Alexander the Third ordered them for the Dowager Empress Maria Feodorovna, the lady Mrs. Aker's great-grandmother worked for and for Alexandra, the Empress, as Easter presents. I have to do some research on the family and the eggs."

"Can you do that online?"

"Online and at the library. But that only tells us what this guy wants, not where the egg is or where Erin is."

Chapter Thirteen

Adam dropped Anne at the library on his way back to his apartment. She walked the short flight of granite steps, noticed again the plaque that identified the octagonal structure as a gift of Andrew Carnegie, and pushed open the heavy oak door. A vision rose of the dead body of the head librarian, a sight that met her the first time she opened that door, years before. Now an assistant, cheerful in spite of having to work Christmas Eve, greeted her.

"I'm looking for a reference work on Fabergé and the Imperial Easter Eggs," Anne said.

"I think we have something upstairs."

They walked up the grey-carpeted stairs to the reference library. The librarian, a pleasant blonde woman named Mrs. Wolfe, remembered her and guided her to the correct area of the holdings. Anne carried the books she chose to one of the scarred oak tables, furnished with a computer every metre or so, that filled the centre of the room. She wanted to scan the diaries of Maria Feodorovna for some clue that she kept one or more eggs in England before she left for Denmark after the first world war. However, the library didn't have a copy in English, and it would be some days before it would arrive on loan. The internet hosted an article that gave some indication of Maria Feodorovna's life before and after the revolution. Soon Anne was lost in the perilous years between the end of the Crimean War and WWI, including the disastrous reign of Nicholas 11.

The story of the Royal Easter Eggs began with Peter Carl Fabergé, a jeweller in St. Petersburg, who took over the family business from his father, Gustav. The Czar, seeing some of Carl's work, had Fabergé jewels displayed in the Hermitage as examples of modern Russian art. He also commissioned Carl to make what would become the first of fifty Easter eggs, fabulous confections of precious metals and jewels. The first egg resembled an ordinary hen's egg, although fashioned from gold, that opened to reveal a golden hen, and yet again to a tiny ruby egg. The Empress was enchanted, and eggs followed most of the years after that. With the coming of the Russian Revolution, many of the eggs were taken to the Kremlin, but some disappeared and were lost to this day. The Soviet government sold several for badly-needed cash. But what of the Dowager Empress? What happened to her private jewels?

A stubborn woman, Maria Feodorovna only fled to the Crimea in 1919. She refused to believe that her family had been murdered and continued to deny it until the end. However, when her nephew, George V of England, sent the HMCS Marlborough for her and her party, she left to take refuge in London with her sister, the Dowager Queen, Alexandra. That didn't last too long, and she moved to Denmark, her childhood home. Likely, Anne thought, some of her jewels went with her, but would she have taken one or more of the Fabergé eggs? One egg had already turned up in America, so why not another?

As with most histories, the lives of the servants weren't included, and Anne wasn't able to confirm Mrs. Akers' story of the escape into exile. Was a Fabergé egg in Culver's Mills? If so, where was it? If Mrs. Akers' family had it, why didn't she know? How had the knowledge been lost? And what about earlier, in 1902 when there was no known order for an Easter Egg? Was there no egg or was there no record? Satisfied that she had learned all she could, Anne closed her laptop, waved to the librarian and left.

Outside, she pulled up the hood of her parka against the wind that blew snow in from the north. Flakes, captured by the fur, melted and dripped onto her face. A small blue car drove by, its driver also muffled against the cold. At the corner the vehicle parked, the engine running. A chill ran through Anne, and her heart beat a rapid tattoo of fear. She hurried across the square and up the few steps to the diner. She slid into a booth next to a window. Her breathing slowed, and she asked for coffee when the server came up to her. The same car crept past the diner and around the corner. What was wrong with her? Why did she think the driver searched for her?

She'd spent a week on the run in Spain, suspicious of every stranger, trusting only the Mossad agent, Daniel. The experience left her with mild PTSD and paranoia was part of that. Or was it a heightened awareness of danger, of noting the things that didn't belong.

Was Quin having her watched? She had a number for him. No answer. She left a message asking him to call.

Later, calmer, Anne walked back to Catherine's through the square dressed for Christmas with fairy lights in the trees and the North Pole scenes in the shop windows. Somehow all the public emblems of joy made her sadder, thinking of Erin, lost with a possible killer and Mrs. Akers, alone in that nursing home where they were prepared to send her when she got ill. And Thomas's mother, who had been so kind to Anne, now struggling with the vagaries of her mind. Thomas. So much stress on him and between them. Somehow, she had to shake off the guilt and remorse of killing Este in Spain. Este would have killed her, killed Naomi. It was a—what did they call it on television—a righteous act. But was it ever righteous to kill?

At a corner, she glimpsed a blue car, perhaps the same one, parked on a nearby street. What was going on? Why hadn't Quin answered? But maybe Pete? Had he somehow decided that she was involved in the kidnapping? No, not Pete. She ran to the gate, pushed it open and raced up the steps. Inside, she slammed the door behind her and shot the bolt.

Her heart thumping, she leaned back against the door for a moment and then walked to the kitchen to put the kettle on. When her tea was ready, she carried it into the library. Outside, Adam's truck pulled up, and he trudged to the door. He looked worn out, Anne thought and more worried than he had been that morning.

"No news?"

"None," he said.

"Do you want some coffee or a drink?"

He sat and rubbed his swollen eyes.

"No. No thanks. What did you learn?"

"I think he wants an Imperial Easter Egg. There's some evidence that the egg went with Maria Feodorovna, the Dowager Empress when the Royal Navy rescued her and took her to Britain. Mrs. Akers' ancestor went on that voyage."

"But she didn't steal the jewellery, the Empress gave it to her."

"So the family story goes. Who knows what happened to the egg? Maybe there isn't one."

Adam rubbed his eyes again. "He wants an imaginary egg?"

"Or a hidden one. Do you know if they police identified the dead woman yet?"

"Pete says her name was Dasha Basanova, wife of a guy called Ivan Basanov. They entered the country on a flight from Toronto to Burlington two weeks ago. Tourists come to ski."

"They must have had help to find out everything they needed to know in two weeks."

"Help from whom?"

"Maybe the Russian government? The Russians claim all the Czarist property as belonging to the state."

The doorbell rang. When Anne answered the door, Pete came in, doffed his police-issue coat and boots, shook hands with Adam, and hugged Anne.

"Any news?"

"Someone saw a van behind the shop late last night. White box-type. Now we're looking for that. You?"

"We think he may want an Imperial Russian Easter Egg that he believes Erin has," said Adam.

Anne came back in with coffee for Pete and a plate of Catherine's ginger cookies.

"Thanks. No lunch," Pete said in apology, grabbing three cookies. "What is an Imperial Easter Egg?"

"The last Czar but one commissioned a jeweller called Fabergé to make gifts for his Empress of exquisite jewelled and enamelled Easter eggs. They are valued highly, in millions of dollars. The Soviet regime sold some and kept others in the Kremlin. Some disappeared."

"Millions for one?" said Pete.

"For one," Anne said.

"So all we have," Adam said, "is a white van, a possible valuable bauble and a dead Russian woman. And maybe a contact person."

"No Russians in town," Pete said.

"And a name. Ivan Basanov. Can we get a passport photo?"

"Sure, but it's the holidays."

"I can sketch him, I think," Anne said. "At least I can try."

"You're staying here alone?"

"No, Thomas is coming."

They left, and Anne swung her feet onto the sofa and drifted off to sleep, waking when the doorbell rang, and Thomas was there.

Chapter Fourteen

Thomas rolled over, reached for Anne, and opened his eyes when he realized she was gone. The smell of coffee and bacon drifted in from the open bedroom door. He dressed and ran downstairs to the kitchen.

She stirred the bacon sizzling in the pan. A multi-coloured apron covered her green sweater and black jeans. Her tousled hair and makeup-free face beamed when she heard his voice.

"Good morning," she said.

"You're up early."

He kissed her neck and sat at the table, looking out at the garden, its features blurred with snow. Footprints led to the bird feeders and back. She'd fed the birds first.

"I'm going to the station to work on a sketch of the man I saw in Erin's shop with the artist they're bringing in from Burlington.

"I'm going back to the house to talk them about Mom. I'll insist on taking her to the doctor."

"Is there someone you can call to see her on Christmas Eve."

"Yes. The staff knows where the funds came from that help keep the doors open at the hospital."

"She's ill and she needs to be seen, endowment or not."

Later, he dropped Anne off in front of the courthouse and drove home. When he stalked into the dining room, he found Claire and Daniel sitting at the oval table that overlooked the rose garden. Cecilia, her arms clutched to her slim figure, stood by the window, close to the dark blue velvet drapes that framed the view.

Beyond, bare stems poked through snow that buried the roses that were their grandmother's pride and summer occupation. Only a few months ago she sat in that garden, waving to him while he talked to Anne about the danger in Spain. Had there been any signs then? Had he missed something? He didn't think so, but he had noticed a change when he returned. Always aware of the feelings of others, always fair and kind, she snapped at him and the young maid. And now, not knowing Anne and sometimes not knowing the girls.

"Grandmama must go to see the doctor," he said.

Cecilia swung around to face him.

"She doesn't want to. I asked her yesterday. She says she's perfectly healthy and she walked all around the garden with the boys," Cecilia said.

What was he going to say to them, Thomas thought. How could he convince them?

Before he could speak, Daniel wiped a weary hand over his face and said, "Did she remember your name?"

"Don't be like that, Danny. She was making a joke when she asked who we all were," Cecilia said.

"Stop deluding yourself," her twin said. "She didn't know us. Something is going wrong."

"She's getting older and Anne being here confused her. Anne said so herself."

Cecilia's proud face, a mirror of her grandmother's, tilted up as she thrust out her jaw.

"Anne was kind. She thinks Grandmama is showing signs of dementia."

"What does she know? She's a children's doctor or was."

Daniel sat back in the chair, the muscles in his jaw tightening, his eyes fixed on his sisters.

"She knows a sick person when she sees one, which is more than I can say for either of you."

Four pairs of dark eyes glared across the table. Conversation stopped when the maid brought in the silver dishes that held eggs and bacon.

"Is Madame up yet?" Cecilia asked.

"No. She hasn't rung yet. Do you want me—"

"No, I'll go."

Moments later, Cecilia's footsteps beat a rapid tattoo on the oak floor of the hall. She stood in the doorway, her face ashen.

"Grandmama's fallen. She won't answer me."

Thomas took the stairs two-at-a-time and raced along the hall to the spacious bedroom that was his mother's. She lay crumpled on the floor, frail and limp. Faint gasping breaths told him she was still alive.

"Call 911, Daniel. She may have had a stroke. Tell them her face is drooping on the left. Cecilia, get a blanket."

"Shouldn't we put—"

"No, she may have hit her head."

Cecilia brought him a soft mohair throw, and he tucked it around his mother's tiny body. When had she become so shrivelled? Why hadn't he noticed? He held her hand, cold and still in his. Claire sat beside him and put her arms around him.

"Do you want me to call Anne?" she said.

"Later, but thank you."

The frivolous French clock on the mantel ticked off the minutes and then tinkled the hour. Ten o'clock. Where were they? His mother stirred a little, moaned, and drifted away again. A siren blared outside the house, and moments later he heard a heavy tread on the stairs. He released his mother to the care of a pony-tailed paramedic and her partner.

"We'll meet you at the hospital," he said.

Claire took his hand. "I called Anne. She's going to the hospital now."

Thomas and Daniel left for the emergency room, leaving the girls to deal with the children and the staff.

∼

After Thomas dropped her off, bundled in her navy parka, Anne climbed the steps of the courthouse, passed the garlanded and beribboned columns, passed the pockmarks left in the wall from the bullets aimed at her years before, and pushed open the heavy oak door. Inside, a glorious Christmas tree, lit with thousands of white lights and hung with silver and gold balls, stood in the centre of the rotunda. What a grand entrance, she thought. A door marked Police Service opened to a work-day world of grey desks, the monotony broken by the colourful screen savers on idle computers.

A young woman, her carrot-red hair tied back, and wearing a regulation navy sweater, stood behind a desk.

Answering her question, Anne said, "I'm Doctor McPhail. Lieutenant Graham wants to see me."

"Please wait."

She sat on a battered oak bench, perhaps a rescue from a renovation in the courthouse. A few moments later, Pete bounded through the outer door.

"Hi, Anne. Come this way."

Pete took her across the squad room to the office that had been Adam's and introduced her to a young woman seated in front of a laptop.

"This is Jenny, our computer artist. She'll work with you to get a likeness of the Russian."

Anne shook the offered hand, noting the paint caught behind the uncoloured nails. An artist in oils as well, she thought.

"I sketched him yesterday after you left. Maybe we can start with that."

She handed her the sketch and sat beside her. The artist chose eyes and ears, lips and nose and built up a composite on the screen.

"His hairline was receding. More, I think, than I sketched and his eyes slightly further apart."

She made the changes, and they worked on.

"That's him," Anne said as the face of the angry customer in the store filled the screen. "That's the man I saw."

Jenny walked to the door and called Pete from the squad room.

"We have it, Lieutenant."

"Great work. Thank you, both. We'll get it out."

Anne left, carrying away her sketch and a copy of the computer-generated image. Pete planned to broadcast the image, on television and the internet. What if Ivan saw it? Would he be more likely to kill Erin or keep her alive to bargain with?

She crossed the square to the diner, sat in a booth and ordered coffee and toast and opened her phone to a news summary. Before she could bring up the site for The Globe and Mail, a Toronto newspaper, the phone rang.

"Anne, can you come to the hospital. Grandmama's had a stroke."

She walked to the hospital and waited in the ER for Thomas to come to her. A medical catastrophe in a family changed everything, all the relationships were stressed, and some never were the same. What would it do to her and Thomas?

Chapter Fifteen

The institution that she supported all her life gathered his mother in and changed her into the patient in the first bed in the resuscitation room. Where was Anne? And then he remembered. They wouldn't let her in because she wasn't family.

"I'm going to find Anne," he murmured to Daniel.

The waiting room, its space filled with light from windows that soared to the second story, held row after row of elderly, pale faces, and young, feverish, red ones. Anne stood apart gazing out the window at the parking lot. Did she still expect him? Wouldn't the staff even tell her they had arrived? He touched her arm, and she turned to him and put her arms around him.

"Anne."

"Oh, Thomas. I'm so sorry. What happened? Claire said her grandmother wouldn't respond. Is she—"

They sat down on the nearest chairs.

"Still alive. The doctors think she stroked and they're transferring her to Burlington for some clot-busting drug."

"Yes. Do you know when she had the stroke?"

"No. She didn't come down to breakfast, and Cecilia found her on the floor."

"Dressed?"

Why was she asking about her clothes? What difference did it make?

"She'd changed. Oh, you mean it must have been after she got ready."

"Yes. How long before you missed her and Cecilia went up?"

He shook his head.

"Too long. We were fighting, and I was glad she missed that."

"So an hour, more, less."

"Why does it matter so much?"

Why did she ask so many questions? All he wanted was for her to be there, a rock at his back.

"The treatment is time sensitive. If the doctors think she stroked during the night, they might think it wasn't worthwhile to treat."

"I'll tell them."

He ran back to the ER door, rang the bell to bring someone to open it, and rushed down the hall to his mother's bed. The family gathered in the doorway.

"What's going on?"

"They seem to be wondering if the transfer would help or hurt her," Daniel said.

Thomas pushed open the door.

"I'm sorry—" the nurse began.

"I need to speak to the doctor about how long it's been since the stroke."

"No one knows—"

"I do. The doctor. Now."

The face that emerged from the curtain was an old friend.

"Still causing trouble, Tom?"

"Alan. Yes. Mom was dressed for the morning, and we found her just inside the door to her room. It can't be longer than two hours now since she had the stroke, likely less."

The doctor asked the nurse how long until the helicopter arrived. Ten minutes she said.

"Flight time an hour?" Thomas asked.

"Yes, with the transfer."

"Will it be in time?"

"Just."

A flight crew in orange jumpsuits burst through the doors and trundled their equipment into the room. Thomas stood aside. The paramedics transferred her, and in a few minutes, she was gone. The girls, wrapped in each other's arms, sobbed. Daniel leaned against the wall beside them, his face stricken with fear.

"Dad."

"I'm going to Burlington; you look after things at home."

He hugged Daniel and the girls and left to search for Anne.

He found her, still standing at the window that overlooked the parking lot and the helipad beyond.

"They've boarded," she said.

"Will you come with me?

"The girls and Daniel—"

"Will come later. I have to be there to give consent and so on."

While he spoke, he took Anne's arm and walked towards the door. Once in the car he leaned back and closed his eyes for a moment. When he opened them, Anne's compassionate eyes met his. He reached over and took her hand. He'd have to resolve the issues with the twins. He couldn't lose her.

Chapter Sixteen

T homas parked in the dedicated lot for Emergency, in front of a Gothic building, astonishing with its pitched roofs and huge chimneys, sitting beside the contemporary hospital.

"What is that? Part of the hospital?"

"No, that's the Converse Building. It's a residence for students at UV."

"Gloomy."

"Haunted, so they say."

They hurried to the emergency room entrance. A few patients and relatives sat on chairs near the information desk where the smiling volunteer directed them to the correct wing. The ER team had admitted her to the Medical ICU and they followed the signs to that building. Anne sat in the light-filled waiting room, expansive with two-story windows and a mezzanine that floated at one end. It was so similar to the hospital in Culver's Mills that she wondered if the same firm had designed them. She stretched her legs to rest them on an ottoman covered in some indestructible orange leather-like material. What if Thomas's mother died? What would that mean for her own relationship with him and with his daughters? Would they blame her for bringing stress into the house?

Across the room, Thomas negotiated with the guardian of access to the ICU, and in a few minutes, the door swung open for him and he disappeared. At the same moment, Claire and Cecilia walked out of the elevator. Cecilia came to her and asked where her father was.

"Inside. The lady at the desk will help you."

"Have you been in?"

"Only family in ICUs."

Cecilia marched over to the desk and spoke to the person there. Claire followed and then trudged back, her jaw, so like Thomas's, set, and said, "Only two at once. What's that about?"

The girls, identical to each other, echoed their father and their grandmother in the planes of their faces that revealed strength and stubbornness both. Somehow, Claire's was softer than Cecilia's.

"Congestion in the ICU, noise, work load. They have lots of reasons. They won't stay long, and you'll be able to go in."

"Cecilia thought everything took too long. She thought they should scoop Grandmama and be out the door."

"They had to stabilize before transport so she could endure the flight."

"I know but Cecilia..."

And they sat, Claire with her eyes on her mobile phone and Anne reading on her Kindle.

"When?" Claire asked.

"It's only been fifteen minutes. Do you want to ask me anything general about stroke?"

"No. I read about it and what this hospital has to offer."

"It's the only level 3 in the state, I think, so it should be state-of-the-art."

"Do you think they will treat her with clot-busting drugs?"

"I think she arrived in time, but the neurologists or the neurosurgeons make that decision. Or the intensivists."

"What are intensivists?"

"ICU specialists."

The elevator doors and Daniel crossed the room to them. He hugged his sister and shook Anne's hand. They kept greeting each other, like characters in a play, Anne thought.

"Any word?"

"None."

The group of three waited a few more minutes and then Daniel went to the desk and asked the receptionist to call his father out for a few minutes.

"Dad, what's going on?"

"They're taking her down for an MRI before they give her the drug."

"Can I see her?"

"I'll bring Cecilia out, and then you and Claire can go in."

Cecilia emerged in front of her father, her face flushed and that jaw set. Identical twins take getting used to, Anne thought. A sense of deja vu.

"Dad said he'd ask if you could go in. I'd rather you didn't."

"Cecilia—"

"It can only confuse my grandmother."

"Our grandmother—"

"Please let it go. I have no intention of going in. It would serve no purpose except to support your father and he would come out if he needed me," Anne said.

"We are supporting our father."

Claire put a hand on her sister's arm.

"Cecilia—"

"Claire, I don't like strangers around when there is family trouble."

Claire sighed and confronted Cecilia.

"Anne is hardly a stranger. After all, she shares Dad's bed when we're not around."

Cecilia drew a breath but held whatever she had to say when Thomas pushed open the door from the ICU.

Anne stood up and walked towards him.

"I think I should go back. I'll rent something—"

"No, you won't. Daniel's going back as soon as she goes for the MRI. You can go with him if you must."

"Cecilia—"

"Yes. I know. We'll talk later."

Twenty minutes later, she leaned back in the seat in Daniel's SUV.

"I'm sorry, Anne."

"Your family keeps apologizing for Cecilia, but does anyone ever confront her?"

"All the time. She's so stubborn."

"Yes, she is."

"I hope you'll stay on. Dad needs you."

"Perhaps."

What did she mean, perhaps? Perhaps she would stay on? Perhaps Thomas needed her? Perhaps she would flee to her home in the north? Her life had been simple before her first visit to Culver's Mills. Would she want to lose all she had gained—the friends, the experiences, good and bad, the excitement, Thomas, to go back to her old life? Perhaps not, but what to do?

Anne hung her coat inside the door of Catherine's home, wishing again that Maggie was there to greet her, tail wagging and tongue giving frantic kisses. She didn't want to be alone with her thoughts.

She wandered into the kitchen and made a cup of tea with milk and found a bag of peanut butter cookies in the cupboard. She carried her cup and two cookies into the library and set them on the table beside her favourite chair.

Not the way she expected to be spending Christmas Eve. Perhaps it was time to go home after all. If Cecilia's attitude poisoned every family holiday, every dinner, every event, how could she stay in Thomas's life? Were they destined to have an off-again, on-again affair, with no commitment and no future?

She hadn't been looking for a relationship when she met him, but her feelings for him had grown. Had his for her? Up until now, she thought so; she thought they were closer.

A storm, blowing up in the last hour, rattled the front windows.

The houses across the road disappeared, leaving only points of colour, their Christmas lights outlining the peaks of the roofs. A car drifted by. Blue, she thought. She was haunted by blue cars. Her phone buzzed on the table where she'd left it. Thomas.

"Hi."

"Are you okay?"

"Yes. No. What is going on? The girls agree to me being there, and then Cecilia carries on like I'm a cuckoo in the nest."

"I'll deal—"

"I don't want you to deal with it. I want to know why and if they can't accept me, who are they going to accept? Do they want you to be alone?"

"I'll come—"

"No. I'll see you in the morning."

"Anne."

"Goodnight."

She held the phone against her forehead for a moment and then sat and looked at the storm and sipped her tea.

Chapter Seventeen

The next morning, Thomas sat at the end of the breakfast table. His children, Daniel to his left, Claire and Cecilia to his right and Olivia, Daniel's wife opposite, in his mother's chair.

"What did you think you were doing yesterday?" he asked Cecilia.

"What?"

"Telling Anne that she couldn't go in to visit Grandmama."

Cecilia flushed and glanced at her twin.

"It would have confused Grandmama."

"She is in a coma. Nothing can reach her at the moment, but it can reach me. Anne is important to me, and I want her with me when we celebrate or when we have troubles. You girls thought nothing of bringing your boyfriends here at Christmas time, but I don't have the same privilege in my own house?"

"But Grandmama—" Cecilia began.

"Likes Anne very much or did before she developed these memory issues. I'm sure she was reacting to the tension from you two."

"Mom—", Cecilia began.

"No. Don't you say what your mother would or wouldn't have

wanted. This is my life we're talking about. Anne will be here any moment. I want her here when we talk about Grandmama's prognosis."

"But—"

"No but's, Cecilia. Keep them to yourself."

The doorbell rang and, moments later, the maid brought Anne to the dining room.

"Good morning," she said, sitting in the chair beside Thomas.

"Good morning. I wanted to talk with the family about my mother's prognosis. Perhaps if there are questions—"

"I'll answer what I can, but remember, adult medicine and certainly neurology, weren't my fields."

The maid came in with a pot of fresh coffee.

"Would you like some breakfast?" Thomas asked.

"No, thank you. Coffee's fine."

"Then I'll tell you all what the doctor said. Grandmama had a severe stroke. They administered the clot-busting drug, but it has only been partially successful. They think perhaps it was too late. If she can get off the ventilator, she will need constant nursing care as well as physiotherapy and speech therapy and so on."

For a moment, no one spoke. Claire reached for Cecilia's hand.

"Why was it too late? Why did they delay?" Cecilia asked.

"They didn't. The delay was here, from the time she got dressed until we missed her."

"That was only a few minutes."

"No. More like an hour. It doesn't matter. What matters is how it has left her and how we can care for her from now on. None of us lives here, and the question is going to be where she is to live. At home or in a facility?"

A babble of voices rose as each of the children spoke. Daniel in his deep baritone, Claire and Cecilia in identical sopranos, each with the same thought. Daniel spoke, his voice drowning out his sisters'.

"We can't warehouse Grandmama."

"It's not a matter of warehousing her. We would choose the best nursing home available. Anne?"

"If you can provide adequate nursing here and ongoing rehab services, if she can benefit from them, her home would be an acceptable alternative. Should she recover more than that, she would need a social environment to help her with speech and behaviour."

"There's nothing wrong with her behaviour," Cecilia said.

"Stroke can change a personality. It depends on where in the brain it happened, the severity of the stroke. And social contact, beyond interacting with a maid and a nurse, is needed to recover. I don't think you can make a decision today, but you need to think of the possibility that she may need to live in an institution."

"Dad, won't you live here if she comes home?" Cecilia said.

"No, I won't. My life and work are elsewhere. I'll be here as often as I can, but she would be alone with her caregivers much of the time."

"Because of Anne," Cecilia said.

"That's enough," Thomas said.

"I'll go," said Anne.

"No—" said Thomas and Daniel.

Anne was up and walking out of the room. Thomas caught her when she waited for her coat.

"Anne—"

"We'll talk later. Go back to them and call me after lunch."

He strode back into the room where his downcast family waited.

"Dad, I'm sorry—"

"You can apologize to Anne later. Right now, we have to decide about Grandmama."

His phone buzzed. A quick glance told him it was Quin.

"This is business, and I have to take it. Talk it over, and we'll discuss what to do later."

He strode out of the room and raised the phone.

"Quin?"

"Ya. Can we meet?"

"I resigned—"

"This is about Anne."

Thomas swung back to the room and told the girls and his son, who sheltered at the other end of the table that he had to go into Culver's Mills.

"Will you be back for lunch?" Claire said.

"Maybe."

Adam's phone, pinging, woke him. He frowned and looked around, wondering where he was. He'd fallen asleep in the shabby chair in the living room, his favourite, that he wouldn't exchange for something new from the shop. The phone pinged again.

Now you have twenty-four hours, cop.

Why?

I want that egg. Get it for me, or she dies.

He called Pete, told him about the text and the revised time. Then he called Anne.

"What's happened?"

"Ivan shortened the time to twenty-four hours."

"Why?"

"Maybe he heard the alert about him. Always a risk."

"Anything back from it?"

"No."

"What more I can do?"

"Keep searching for that damn egg."

"I will."

After he clicked off, Adam paced the apartment, touching the objects Erin loved: the art deco lamp with a stained-glass, Tiffany shade, her mother's picture, their engagement picture from Bermuda. She was tough; her childhood with an alcoholic father had ensured that. She would survive. He circled the room again.

But he couldn't stay in the apartment, not without her. He waded through the fresh snow to the courthouse and the police station that shared the space with the court.

He hesitated a moment before pushing open the oak door that separated the courthouse from the police station. Could he help?

Would he have wanted the family to interfere if he still had the job? No. He passed through, said hello to the receptionist, and made his way across the squad room, stopping at first one desk and then another to shake a hand, say thanks, to the corner office that used to be his. The blinds were up and the door open. Pete's long legs rested on the battered desk. He hadn't changed much in the office, Adam thought, except the diploma on the wall and the picture on the desk, now his wife instead of Erin.

Erin. The loss hit him at unexpected times in awkward places, like a belly blow. He took a breath and knocked on the door frame. Pete swung his legs off the desk, stood up and pulled a visitor chair close to his.

"You're pale, man. Sit, sit."

"Yeah, comes and goes."

Adam sat and put his head in his hands for a moment and straightened his back.

"Any progress?" he asked.

"No".

"What the hell? No one noticed the van? No camera footage anywhere? What about the phone calls? How many guys you got working on it?"

Adam stood and prowled the small space.

"All of them. You know that. We all want to bring Erin home. FBI too, with lab work but without any evidence that the kidnapper crossed a state line, that's about it. Sit, sit."

"We know the territory better."

"Extra hands would be good."

"You got mine."

"I don't know how the boss will feel about a victim's relatives—"

"Come off it, Pete. I'm staying so you might as well use me."

"But the Sheriff—"

The phone, ringing, interrupted him. When he hung up, he said, "A break. A gas station camera picked up a white van going north. The driver looks like this Ivan."

"North. Where the hell is he going? He can't cross the border."

"Mountains."

Mountains. North of Culver's Mills, hills gave way to the Green Mountains that gave the state its nickname. Difficult to search, especially with snow filling the roads and trails. What if she escaped? He dragged her on that winter survival course last year. Would she remember enough? Pete was on the phone again.

"Get that picture out."

"Do we know anything more about this guy?" Adam said.

"Not much."

"Do we know where they were staying?"

"Yeah, just now. That motel on the highway beside the warehouses."

"Searched?"

"Not yet. I'm going out."

"I'll follow—"

"Nah, ride with me. If something comes in, you'll hear it too."

In the parking lot, they climbed into Pete's truck, a Ford 150, and headed west to the highway north. On the way, Pete turned on the local radio station. A bulletin alerted the public to the white van and its possible role in a kidnapping. Pictures on the internet site, the announcer said, of the victim and the man who was wanted for questioning.

Pete took the quick left to Commerce Road off the highway. There was a motel hidden among the small factories and shops of the industrial area.

You had to know it was here, Adam thought, but Pete knew the town better than anyone. The Russian must have spent some time scouting the area to find it. There were only two cars, one by the manager's office, the other further along in front of unit three. A red-tiled roof gave the place its name - Red Roof Inn. A row of vending machines with the usual - chips, pop, chocolate bars - marked the manager's office, an afterthought tacked to the end of the row of stuccoed units. Last time he'd been out here, rust from dripping eves stained the stucco. A recent paint job had covered those. Pete nosed the truck into a space in front of the motel's office.

"Changed hands again," he said. "New people from St. Alban's."

"That explains the paint and new shingles."

Adam watched him question the owner, pick up a key, shake the man's hand, and come out to the truck. He rolled down the window.

"Unit five. Gloves in the box."

Adam pulled on a pair of latex gloves. Maybe they'd find something, anything, pointing to where the guy took Erin. Maybe.

Chapter Eighteen

On the way into Culver's Mills, Thomas emptied his mind of the confrontation with the girls. High banks, covered with fresh snow, lined the road to town. He pulled off for a moment to let a plough with its flashing light pass. Brown slush covered the pristine snowbanks in its wake.

Over the years, he'd learned to keep his normal life—the family, his business, love affairs—separate from whatever he did for the CIA. But Quin being in Culver's brought it all too close. Why this hole-in-the-wall meeting in a park instead of at the office Thomas kept in the town? He passed through the quiet square, drove along the pond past the weir and slotted his car in beside a grey sedan in the lot beside the old mill. After a few moments, when sure that he was unobserved, he got out and climbed into the passenger seat of the other vehicle. Quin offered a hand, and he shook it.

"Best of the season, Tom."

"Same to you, but why are we here?"

"Anne is here, at Catherine's B&B?"

Thomas clenched his jaw and shifted in his seat to look at Quin's face. Blank, as always, giving nothing away.

"Yes. So?"

"So maybe she should stay with you."

"Why?"

It wasn't like Quin to interfere in another agent's life or even his work. Quin scanned the surroundings every few seconds. Watching, but for whom?

"You remember Colette?" Quinn said, bringing his eyes back to Thomas.

"The Swiss woman who handled the kidnappers in Spain, the ones who tried to kill Anne. Oh, yeah. I remember her."

"Yes. Colette. She's here, and I think she's after Anne."

Thomas took a deep breath before he answered.

"In Culver's Mills? What would a Swiss woman, an agent of gunrunners, want here? What have you done?"

Quin looked past him and down the path beside the pond.

"What? Nothing. We think she's working for the Russians and controlling the thieves who hit Erin's shop, maybe the kidnapper. And that she wants personal revenge."

"Revenge? Come on, Quin. On who? You?"

"Not me. I'm not the one who interfered in Bermuda, who spoiled her operation in Spain. Anne."

Thomas sagged back into the seat.

"She wants to kill her?"

"We think so."

What was he going to do? Anne was barely speaking to him.

"Thanks for the warning. I'll convince her to stay with me."

Thomas reached to open his door.

"Wait, Tom. She won't be safe unless we take Colette down and we need Anne to draw her out."

He let go of the handle and rotated back to Quin.

"A target? You want to make her a target, again. She's a doctor, not an agent."

"We'll keep her safe. You know—"

"I know we owe you."

Quin saved Anne's sister's life in Bermuda and gave them information in Spain that helped them recover Anne and the kidnapped child.

"It's not that. Anne will never be safe unless we take Colette down. Never, Tom. The woman's implacable."

"I'll talk to her. What do you want to do?"

"Put her under surveillance and put information out that she has the jewels."

"I'll try."

"Do you want me—"

"No."

Thomas opened the door and stepped out to see Anne's astonished face.

~

Earlier that day, after the confrontation with Thomas's children, Anne waited in the hall for the maid to bring her coat. The paintings on the walls always intrigued her, changing as they did from one visit to the next. Sometimes Claire's taste prevailed, sometimes her grandmother's. The grandmother's this time, she thought: an exquisite icon of Mary and her child, a copy of Raphael's *The Miraculous Draught of Fishes*.

Once in her car, she sat for a moment, her eyes focussed on the blue door. She gave herself a shake. What did she expect? That he would run after her? She shoved the stick into first gear and stepped on the gas, spinning the wheels on the gravelled drive.

The trip into Culver's took only ten minutes. Anne concentrated on the road, fighting to keep anger at Thomas's children from taking over her mind. What about the art? Madame Beauchamp was a religious woman. The paintings had meaning for her beyond that of a connoisseur. Anne's thoughts drifted to the iconography of Christian art. The fish was an enduring symbol in ancient and modern imagery, from Raphael onward. Based on an acrostic of the initials in the Greek words for Jesus Christ, early Christians used the symbol to identify themselves. She shook her head. Why was she thinking about fish when her life was crashing once again?

She left the car at Catherine's to walk and sort out her feelings and her future. The winter storm of the night before left the narrower streets in the older part of town clogged with vehicles, fantastic shapes, like weird beasts under their blanket of white. She trudged along the road, avoiding the invisible and treacherous sidewalks until she passed the park near the mill-pond where a sidewalk plough had made a single pass.

Two cars sat in the parking lot, their roofs clear of snow. One was empty, the other with a driver who resembled Quin from the back. Something to do with his mysterious mission, she supposed. As she passed, the passenger door opened, and Thomas stepped out. Her eyes met his, she swivelled, and rushed down the path into the park. Why was he with Quin? He said he was through with him and the CIA. At the water's edge, she stopped. Or rather, she thought, the ice-edge. If the harsh winter continued, they had talked skating on New Year's Day. Now... Or was she over-reacting? They were old friends. Why shouldn't they meet?

"Anne."

She turned to his voice.

"I'm sorry I ran away like that. It was foolish."

"Not so foolish. Listen to what Quin wants you to do. Walk with me. "

The ploughed section of the path ended, and they took to the road towards Catherine's. For long minutes, Thomas said nothing. Anne put her hand on her arm. His muscle tensed under her fingers, relaxed, tensed again.

"What does he want me to do?"

"He wants you to stay. I told him how things were with my family and that you might go back to Toronto. He assumed you would be staying to hunt for Erin and I reminded him that you were a doctor, not an agent."

"Why does he want me to stay?"

Thomas hesitated, and then said, "He thinks you will draw Colette out."

Anne's voice rose.

"He wants me to be a target, a tethered goat. To put my life at risk, again, for some CIA operation that's illegal anyway in this country."

"We owe him. From Europe, we owe him."

"Do we owe him my life."

"No, never that. We'd both protect you. You know that."

"It hasn't worked before."

Anne stalked away from him, her shoulders hunched against the cold, her hands thrust deep into her pockets.

∼

Thomas took a step after her but hesitated and walked back to the car where Quin waited.

Quin rolled down his window.

"What did she say?"

"That we failed to protect her before. Then she walked away."

Quin shook his head.

"What will she decide?"

"I don't know. Whatever she thinks is the right thing to do, and there is more than Colette to consider. Erin's still missing."

"I imagine she's dead."

"You would."

"Let me know if she stays."

"Maybe."

Thomas watched for a moment as Quin drove away. Should he go to her? He opened the door of his car. His phone was ringing.

Daniel. A jolt of fear hit his chest, and he gripped the wheel with his free hand.

"Yes?"

"Dad, the hospital called. They think she's getting worse and—"

"What do they mean by worse?"

Quin waved a hand as he turned into the street.

"I don't know. Less responsive, I think. They want to talk to you, to us, about resuscitation orders."

What was he going to do? What chance was there for her and what did the deterioration of the last few weeks mean?

"Did you mention that to the girls?"

"Yes. Cecilia exploded, but Claire is more reasonable."

"And you?"

"I don't know, Dad. What if we say no resuscitation and she could have recovered?"

"I'll be out to the house in a little while. And Danny, I hope Anne will come with me and I want her treated with respect."

"Okay, I'll tell them."

He needed to talk to Anne but would she even see him now. She was so angry, white with anger. He turned the key in the ignition. He'd go to Catherine's and try.

Chapter Nineteen

Anne fled towards the square. What was she going to do? It was no use Thomas saying that they would protect her. She didn't believe that. Colette would come for her, to kill her. She should go home.

But would going home solve the problem? If Colette wanted revenge, she could find out where she lived. Nothing easier. And then what? She would be on her own.

Not so easy to obtain a gun in Canada but not impossible if Colette wanted to shoot her. There were other ways of killing. Her mouth went dry, and her heart pounded. Panic again. She stopped her forward rush and waited, breathed, willed herself to be calm. When her heart rate slowed, she crossed the square towards Erin's shop, pausing in front of the heroic stature of the town's founder. Generations had rubbed the toe of his boot to a bright copper. She touched it and walked to the corner where Erin's store stood in darkness. Anne looked past the decorations in the window to the interior, bereft in Erin's absence.

What should I do? If she left, she couldn't help with the search for Erin, but what good would she do in that? Only the resources of the police were going to make any difference.

Her face, hidden within the fur that outlined the hood of her parka, reflected in the window. The woman in the window, pale, eyes wide-open, shining with tears. What should she do? If she left, she would be abandoning Erin, giving up on her. She would lose Adam's friendship. What about Thomas? He didn't want her to do this, but he thought they should help Quin because he helped them. And Quin had saved her sister from the assassin in Bermuda. What about Thomas? His life was upside down with his mother dying and his daughters needing so much support in their fear of losing the grandmother who helped raise them. He needed her, and she couldn't abandon him.

What about her struggle with PTSD? Would staying to help Erin and Thomas make it worse or better? It wouldn't matter if Colette killed her.

She shivered, the cold creeping past her coat, into her bones. Time to go.

She slogged through the snow to Catherine's home. When she turned the corner, she saw that someone sat on the front porch. Fear grabbed her and held her but then the figure waved, and she knew it was Thomas. She hurried on, slipping as she went through the gate in her rush to get to him.

"Thomas, I—"

"Anne—"

They laughed but then Thomas's pale face and worried eyes told her something more was wrong.

"What is it?"

"They want to talk about a DNR order for my mother. Will you come to the house with me to talk to the family?"

"Yes, but—"

"I told Daniel what I expect from them."

"All right. Now?"

"If you can?"

"Of course."

They drove in silence to the old stone house by the lake. The brief trip took them past manor-like homes, set back from the highway by snow-covered lawns and fields, many of them enclosed by horse fences. No horses grazed in the pastures on the bitterly cold day. A lone black Labrador retriever stood guard outside a barn.

When they turned into the drive, the blue door opened, and Daniel stepped out.

"Has something happened?"

"No. I wanted to tell you I talked to the girls and there won't be any problem."

The men in this family were used to being in charge, Anne thought. They left their coats in a heap on a chair in the hallway and walked into the dining room.

~

The blue Chevrolet Cruze idled down the street from where Colette's enemy lived. Soon McPhail would appear and then it would be over. She glanced at the clock on the dashboard. Fifteen minutes. A winter jogger, a slow-paced figure in bright red and black passed and a few moments later trotted back again and stopped at the car. She tapped at the window.

"Are you having some trouble, ma'am?" the jogger said when Colette rolled down the window. A fair, pretty face with dark blue eyes looked into hers.

"No, waiting."

A slight frown creased the smooth forehead.

"You're pumping a lot of carbon monoxide into the air."

"Pardon," said Colette at her most French.

"You're not from here. We have a local ordinance that forbids idling the car for more than ten minutes. I noticed you when I went out twenty minutes ago. You must shut the engine off."

What was this? Who was this woman? A police spy? Talking about carbon monoxide? Stupid.

"Pardon?"

"Shut off the motor or I'll call the police."

She wasn't police. Colette rolled up the window and ignored the tapping. Would she call the police on such a trivial matter? The jogger run up the steps of a house across the street and pulled out her phone.

Merde. She was. She would have to move the auto and miss a chance again. She cruised past the B&B. Who was that? A man sat on the porch, in the cold, watching the street as she had. Was he Ivan? No. Too dark and too well-dressed. As she turned the corner, she glanced back. A woman, head down, stomped through the snow on the sidewalk and turned in at the gate. McPhail. Colette pounded the steering wheel. Too late. Too late to kill her today. Later, she would search the house for the egg and wait for the McPhail. And it would be done.

Chapter Twenty

The next morning, Ivan sat at the table, shovelling yet more eggs and bacon into his mouth. Between mouthfuls, he sent a text.

"Are you sure he loves you, this cop?"

"Yes."

"He hasn't got the egg yet. So now I said twenty-four hours. Before tomorrow morning."

"But—"

"But what? I gave too much time before."

"I told you where the jewellery is."

"Not the egg."

Erin pounded her fists on the table, knocking over his coffee. The black liquid crept across the table towards him.

"I never had an egg. Never."

"Clean up this mess. I'm going to the town, to that house where the woman is staying."

"What woman?"

"That woman, that Anne. You said she had the jewellery. Maybe I will bring her here, and you can watch until you tell me what I want to know."

He dragged her from the chair and hurled her away from him.

Her right hand hit the floor. Pain shot up to her shoulder. Was it broken? She rotated her wrist. No, not broken. She mopped the floor with a towel he threw down at her and pulled herself up with her left hand. When she finished cleaning, he stood behind her with a hammer.

"What—"

Her mouth was dry, her tongue too big for her mouth.

"Go in the bedroom."

He followed her in, swinging the hammer. Her back twitched with fear, but when she turned, he was smiling.

"I'm going, and you are staying. You are in the mountains, and the storm is coming. If I return without the egg..."

Erin collapsed on the bed. He glowered at her and left. The door locked behind him and he nailed something. Nailed her in. What if he didn't return? What if he died on the road or in a shoot-out or decided to take the jewellery and run. What if a fire broke out? What would she do?

The outer door to the cabin slammed, and she heard the roar of the van's engine. He said they were in the mountains. Which mountains? Vermont has so many.

Her breathing slowed, and her pounding heart quieted. She surveyed the room, tried the door. He'd been thorough. Why was there no window? What kind of a place had a bedroom with no window.

She was hungry too. She had swallowed another raw egg and wolfed a few pieces of bacon when he made her cook for him again, but they wouldn't last long. She lay down on the bed, trying not to think of Anne and what Ivan might do to her. After a while, she realized she focussed on one corner of the ceiling.

A square of plywood interrupted the rough-hewn boards. A trap door. But she had nothing to climb on. No chair, no table, only the bed. Would she be strong enough? She dragged and pushed the bed across the room until it stood under the trap door. The wooden headboard might let her reach it if she could balance, but she was weak from the beatings and lack of food.

She pulled herself onto the headboard and balanced. Her hands reached the plywood and pushed. The board gave way, falling out of the opening, glancing off her shoulder. She grabbed at the edge and held on. It was an attic, an attic with a pull-down stair. She collapsed on the bed. Now to climb up and hope there was a way out.

Boarded. Floorboards extended the length of the cabin. At one end, a window let in some light. Bent over in the space that was too low even for her, Erin crept across the boards until she reached the window. Outside, snow-laden spruce blocked the view of the mountains. Below, drifts against the house rose almost half-way up the outside wall. She ran her hands around the window. No catch, no way to open it. She'd have to break it.

She dragged a quilt from the bed below—Boston Embassy pattern, she noted automatically— across the boards, wrapped part of it around her arm and more over her head and hit the window. Not hard enough. She took a breath, covered her head and smashed the glass with her elbow. A satisfying rain of shards flew around her and tinkled on the floor. She cleared away the remaining fragments of glass.

Snow swirled around her as the wind found the open window. She could throw the quilt and the other blankets out the window too, enough to cover the broken glass. She waited for a lull in the gusts and dropped the quilt. It lay a little beyond where she thought she would land when she jumped.

She climbed down the stairs and back up with the sheets and another blanket, an old Hudson Bay from Canada with its cheerful red and green and cream stripes, and added them to the pile below. Surely most of the glass was covered now. She wrapped her hands in pillowcases, clutched the sides of the window and pulled herself up and through. No time to think. She let go and fell into the pile of fabric and snow below.

Chapter Twenty-One

Maddy lounged in the battered, green and orange plaid lazy-chair, her feet hooked over one arm, her back against the other. A news bulletin interrupted her television programme. She swung her legs to the floor, squinted at the television, and shouted to her grandfather.

"Grandpa, Grandpa."

The urgency in her voice brought him in from the kitchen. He stood in the doorway, coffee in hand.

"What?"

"On the tv. Isn't that the guy who rented the cabin? The mean one?"

"What's his face up there for?"

"The police want to talk to him about a woman who disappeared from Culver's Mills. You have to call them."

Maddy scribbled on her notebook until the message left the screen.

"I don't know. They ain't our business."

"Yes, it is. What if he has her up at the cabin? What if he's hurting her?"

Her grandfather's face held that stubborn expression that meant his mind was made up, but Maddy tried again.

"What if it was me up and someone else didn't help. All we have to do is call. Please, Grandpa or I'll get Nick, and we'll go."

Her grandfather sighed.

"Never you mind that. I'll call."

"Now? I wrote down the number."

She passed him her school notebook, with the phone number for Culver's Mills police scribbled on the cover. He picked up the phone and dialled.

∼

The smell hit Adam first—junk food and sweat, stale coffee and cheap perfume. Clutter spread from one end of the room to the other: pizza boxes with left-over slices stacked on a table; dirty clothes heaped in a corner; papers tumbled on the bed. Adam checked the documents while Pete searched the rest of the room.

"A map here."

"Of what?"

"This part of the state. Detailed, with a route marked out going south."

"South? Why would he go south? Too settled."

"You know that, but does he?"

"Anything else?"

"A bunch of clippings about the Russian Imperial Easter Eggs. An article about Romanov genealogy. One of the names is circled. Maybe this guy believes he is a descendent?"

"Or knows who is?"

Pete took the map and papers and stuffed them in an evidence bag.

"You don't think we should extend the alert south?" Adam said.

"Didn't say that. Doubt it will help."

Pete's phone buzzed.

"Graham."

Pete listened without a word. When he clicked off, Adam asked what was going on.

"Guy came in. Said he rented a cabin to someone who looked like our sketch. Let's go."

Minutes later they left the town behind and took the highway north.

"North, not south?"

"Yeah. Heard the FBI was sniffing around, asking about you."

"I'm considering it but, if I got posted somewhere else, that would up uproot Erin."

"That likely?"

"Yeah."

"What instead?"

"General law, here in Culver's Mills. Hagerty asked me to come in with him when I pass the bar exams."

"Does the FBI want you to pass the bar?"

"I want to. It gives me more options."

"You're not getting any younger."

"I want to go back to policing, but Erin had a hard-enough time with that when she had a home and a business, friends, a life in Culver's. How will she feel if we have to move across the country?"

"She'll make friends. Everyone likes Erin."

"Yeah."

They drove in silence for long minutes, the road winding through rolling hills. Dense clouds obscured the summit of Mount Mansfield to the east. Snowing up there, Adam thought.

Vermont's landscape, here in the north of the state, varied from mountains dotted with ski hills to the northeast to lakes, their shores built up with vacation homes and resorts. Dense forest covered much of the mountainous areas. Ivan could hide her in there for days, weeks maybe.

"Where's this cabin?"

"Below the mountain and a little north."

"Road may not be ploughed."

"We'll stop to talk to the owner."

Pete drove down a long lane to a green frame house nestled in a grove of pine trees. A black dog, with a wagging tail and one white ear flopped down, and the other standing straight up, loped across the yard to meet them, barking. Behind him, a quiet German Shepherd, stood, watching. Pete and Adam waited.

The door of the farmhouse opened and a thin, stooped man, about sixty, red hair fading into grey and a deep farmer's tan on his face, whistled the dogs to him and ambled with them to the truck.

"Yup?"

"Culver's Mills police," said Pete, showing his identification. "You called about renting a cabin to the guy on the news."

"Yup."

"Where's the cabin?"

The man unfolded a hand-drawn map and passed it to Pete.

"How long ago?"

"Two days."

"How's the road?"

"Passable."

"Thanks."

"Yup."

Adam checked the map. The route would take them thirty miles into the hills. Pete put the truck in gear, waved to the farmer and drove back down the lane.

Fifty minutes later they reached the road to the cabin.

"New tracks at the gate," Pete said.

"Walk in?"

"Yeah."

Pete took a shotgun from the back and handed it to Adam.

"I'm armed," Adam said.

"Now you're better armed."

Erin lay for a moment on the sheets and blankets that covered the glass and snow. Nothing hurt. The wind howled around her, blowing snow into her eyes. She gathered the bedclothes to protect her from the storm and struggled through the thigh-high drifts to the door of the cabin. Would it be locked? Maybe he thought nailing the door to her room was enough. She turned the handle and pushed. The door yielded, and she stumbled through into the warmth of the stove. Pain knotted her stomach. She needed food and water, but bacon and eggs and toast and coffee would take too long. She'd left a jar of jam and piece of butter on the counter. She spread them on a thick slice of bread and wolfed them down. But she had to escape before he came back. There was no imperial egg for him to find and he would take his fury out on her.

The main room of the cabin was given over to the kitchen, a couple of broken-down sofas and, in one corner, a door. Inside a closet, she found a collection of boots and snowshoes and even an old parka. The parka smelled of sweat and mould, but it would protect her from the snow. So would the winter overalls hung up beside it. Were they Ivan's? She pulled them on and stuffed the trailing cuffs into a pair of worn work boots.

How she wished she'd paid more attention in that survival course Adam took her on. But she knew she'd need matches and something to carry water or a can to melt water, and food and more socks. But she didn't have more socks. She cut up sheets to wrap her feet and crammed more in the too-big boots until they fit. She gathered matches and a lighter from the shelf above the stove, a discarded coffee can from the garbage, and more bread from the fridge. She stowed as much as she could carry in a canvas bag and tied the remaining sheet to it to make straps for a backpack.

She opened the door to a wall of falling snow that stung her eyes. She needed the sunglasses and identification and the miniature Swiss knife she kept in her purse. She stowed them in the pack and stepped out. Outside the cabin, she strapped on the snowshoes and put one cautious foot after another forward into the snow and wind. Which way? She had no idea, but she needed to go while it was still snowing so her tracks would fill in. She'd walk until the light faded and then she'd hide, somewhere.

Chapter Twenty-Two

At the Beauchamp home, early on Christmas Eve, Daniel and his sisters sat around the oval mahogany table, covered now with a white linen tablecloth set for tea. A triangle of sandwich and a lone grape tomato decorated Claire's plate. Her mood reflected in her face, drawn and dark-eyed. Cecilia stood up when Thomas and Anne came in, held out a hand to Anne, not to shake it, but to hold while she wrapped her other arm around Thomas.

In the background, Claire sniffled, and Daniel stared out at the rose garden, shrouded with snow.

"Dad, Anne, I'm sorry."

"Please don't—" Anne said.

"We have to talk," said Thomas. "Anne and I are on our way to Burlington. You all know what the doctors are asking. I have to decide what to tell them."

"What does it mean? What will they do?" said Claire.

"Anne?" he said.

Thomas held out a chair for her beside him, and she sat down opposite the twins. Daniel took his grandmother's place at the head of the table.

"First, a do not resuscitate order instructs the staff not to begin a rescue procedure. They will stand by and allow death to occur. That is all it means for now."

"For now?" Daniel asked.

"If she survives her stroke but is unable to swallow, at some point they may ask you about tube feeding. That is a decision for another day. If you don't allow a DNR, if her heart or breathing stops, they will institute a full cardiac arrest procedure, including heart compressions and intubation and ventilator use. That has its risks, from fractured ribs to the consequences of lack of oxygen to her brain, depending on how long the resuscitation takes. If she is ventilated, at some point, they will try to wean her off. That may fail, and ventilation will have to continue, or you may have to decide to turn it off."

Three shocked faces told her she had given too much information, too soon.

"Right now, you must decide if you want her to have a full cardiac arrest procedure or not. Has anyone had a conversation with her about end-of-life issues?"

"One day," Claire began, "we were watching something on PBS about living wills. She said she intended to do one but hadn't yet."

"Did she tell you her views?" Thomas said.

"She said she would only want to survive if her life would continue as it had been."

"But she didn't define that?"

"Not to me."

"She told me she was glad to have lived long enough to see her great-grandchildren. That was before she didn't recognize us anymore."

Cecilia put her hands over her face and sobbed.

"What do you think, Dad?" Daniel said.

"I want to listen to what you think before I make a decision."

"Don't you mean before we make a decision?" Cecilia said.

"No. I hold Mom's power of attorney for personal care."

"We all get a vote—"

"It's not a land deal, Cecilia. No vote," said Daniel.

"But—"

"I have to decide for all of us."

"Anne, what do you think?" said Claire.

"I think you should consider what gave her joy and if she will be able to carry on experiencing that joy if she has severe handicaps. When Thomas talks to the doctors, they will give him their opinion on her prognosis, and he can go on from that point."

"When are you going?" Daniel asked.

"Now. Anne is coming so I ask the right questions. I don't want all of you to come—"

"Could I?" said Cecilia. "I want to hear what they have to say."

"Recognizing that it is my decision. I don't want a scene, Cecee."

"Yes."

Chapter Twenty-Three

After Thomas and Cecilia spent a few minutes at his mother's bedside, they joined Anne in the visitor's sitting room off intensive care. Comfortable chairs, upholstered in the faded green that hospital designers thought was calming, surrounded a pecan-wood coffee table. A silver urn stood on a matching credenza, balanced by an autumn bouquet of flowers in burnt orange and pale yellow.

The doctor, a man about fifty years old, with dark, worried eyes and a severe mouth, sat opposite Anne and a younger man, an intern or resident, Thomas supposed, stood beside his chair. No one spoke until Thomas did.

"Doctor Patton? I'm Thomas Beauchamp. My daughter, Cecilia. My friend, Doctor McPhail."

He acknowledged the introductions with a nod.

"I understand you want to talk about a DNR order. What can you tell us about my mother's prognosis?"

"As you know, we attempted to reverse the effects of the stroke with drug therapy and were successful in clearing the clot. However, significant lack of oxygen to that area of the brain had occurred. Your mother has profound weakness on the right side, and at the moment, she hasn't recovered enough to be taken off the ventilator. We were able to do an MRI when she arrived and those results coupled with her progress are what I want to talk to you about today."

Thomas listened to the authoritative, cool voice describe the damage to his mother's brain. Cecilia sat beside him, and he took her hand. She grasped it the way she had when she was little, her fingers encircling his thumb. Her grandmother had taken the place of her mother when his wife died.

"The initial MRI revealed an extensive area of damage from the clot, but it also showed evidence of multiple small strokes in different areas of the brain. Had she been showing symptoms for some time of memory loss or personality change?"

"Yes," said Thomas. "I was away in Spain in the early part of the fall. When I returned in October, I noticed she was more irritable with the household staff. After that, she rapidly lost memory, forgetting people and relationships. New losses occurred almost daily."

"But she remembered us sometimes," Cecilia said.

"Cecee, she thought you were your mother, and the children were you and Claire."

Cecee's face fell, and she hid her face in her father's jacket.

"What do you need from us today, Doctor?" said Anne.

"A decision about what you want us to do if her heart stops. Her cardiac rhythm is abnormal—atrial fibrillation that has been unresponsive to therapy so far. As well, she remains on the ventilator, and at some point, we will attempt to wean her off. Did she leave an advance directive."

"She spoke to her maid but not to us," Cecilia said.

Her voice broke, and she squeezed Thomas's hand.

"Nothing in writing?"

"No."

"I hold her power of attorney for personal care," Thomas said.

He withdrew a document from his briefcase, removed it from its envelope and handed it to the doctor.

"When she made it out, all she said was that she didn't want to survive if she wouldn't be herself, if she were unable to do the things she enjoyed. What I need to know from you is how likely is she to recover most of her lost abilities."

"I think unlikely to."

"Doctor, I think the family needs to understand that this doesn't mean any active measures will be taken to shorten her life, that it means only that your staff won't initiate a resuscitation procedure if her heart stops. Other decisions, such as weaning her off the ventilator and feeding tubes will be taken later, I presume," Anne said.

"That's correct."

"How can you be so clinical?" Cecilia said to Anne. "What if she were your mother? Would you be so hard-hearted then?"

"Cecilia—"

"No, Dad," she said. "It's not her decision."

"I didn't say anything about my making the decision, Cecilia. And it is heartrending to tell the staff to stop when you get a midnight call. It is far better they know in advance what to do. I'll leave you to it, shall I?"

She stood up, but Thomas took her hand.

"No, Anne. Please stay. You know what the technical information means, and I want your advice, and for that, you need to hear what the doctor says."

"But Dad—"

"You may remember that you promised, Cecilia."

Thomas glanced across at the doctor and his resident. They waited, he thought. Through all these family scenes, they waited, knowing they had to decide at the moment when death occurred. He wouldn't give the order to stop a resuscitation, nor would his children, but that young man, quietly listening, would.

"Physical resuscitation is quite—" His voice faltered, and he was grateful when the doctor picked up the sentence.

"Hard on the patient and may not succeed in any event. More damage to the brain may happen at that time as well."

"Anne?"

"The prognosis is so poor, Thomas, and she is so frail."

"Then I have decided that at this time, with her poor prognosis for recovery of her faculties as she would want them, you should not resuscitate if her heart stops."

"Dad—"

"Enough."

"I wanted to say that I agree."

Thomas put his arm around her, and she cried into his jacket. The doctor nodded, and he and his young follower left. A few moments later, Anne and Thomas and Cecilia walked to the elevator and out to the car.

He'd go home, Thomas thought, to go through it all again with Claire and Daniel.

~

The trip back to Culver's Mills was thick with silence. The snow still fell. The wiper blades moved across the windshield, clicking in their metronomic fashion. An old song ran through Anne's head, something about an old man's clock, ticking away his life, stopping when he died.

She glanced at Thomas. He sat forward, peering into the snow but his hands on the wheel were relaxed. She would be white-knuckled, Anne thought. She was always nervous in the snow, and since a murderous driver forced her off the road in the midst of a snowstorm, the fear was worse. But Thomas was calm, and the trip took only a few minutes longer than usual.

Inside the house, the maid bustled around, removing coats and asking about drinks or food. Thomas told her they would sit in the morning room.

Thomas sat the head of the table, silent until the maid finished bringing in a trolley with coffee and drinks. His family waited, Anne at his right, Daniel at the end of the table, the girls side by side on the left. His wife was with the children, Daniel said. They were always meeting in this space, Anne thought. When she first saw it, she loved the polished, antique charm of the mahogany table with the view of the rose garden in summer, but now, the room seemed full of the family's pain.

"What did you decide, Dad?" Daniel said, leaning towards his father.

"First I'll tell you what the doctor said. Grandmama had a catastrophic stroke and the efforts to reverse the damage failed although they did clear the clot. Her brain showed evidence of many small prior strokes."

Anne listened as he reviewed all the doctor told them. The faces around the table held the shocked expression she knew so well. So much to process, especially if one had no medical knowledge at all.

Daniel, his eyes intent on his father's face, Claire, her hands twisting and writhing, as if they had a life of their own, beyond her control, Cecilia, who cried throughout the trip back from Burlington and whose face now looked numb: what were they thinking?

"Dad, what did you decide?" Daniel said again, his voice strained.

"I decided that if her heart stopped or if she failed to wean off the ventilator, we would let her go. She would have no peace if I forced her to live as a profoundly-damaged person."

"What did you think, Anne?"

Claire's voice held an echo of the timid child she must have been.

"I think that Thomas made the only decision possible, but you must understand that there may not be a moment when the DNR order comes into effect. She may wean off the respirator; she may respond to treatment of her heart condition. The decision may not be how she will die but how she will live."

"Could she come home?"

"If she weans off the respirator, if she can undergo rehabilitation, she may be able to come home, but the nursing burden will be heavy. If she is bed-ridden, she may need four or more caregivers, as well as ongoing visits from physiotherapists, occupational therapists, speech pathologists. She may not be able to swallow and need a gastric tube or a direct feeding tube into the stomach. Caring for her here may be difficult if those services are not locally available."

"What will we do, Dad?" Cecilia asked.

"Deal with what comes. As for right now, Grandmama is on a respirator; she has a feeding tube; she is sedated. Tomorrow or the day after, they will try to wean her off the machine. We'll know better then."

"What do you think her chances are?" said Claire, looking to Anne.

"I'm not qualified to make that call, even if I had all her medical records in front of me," Anne said.

"Should we stay longer?" said Daniel.

"For a day or so after Christmas if you can."

Cecilia thumped her fists on the table.

"How can we sit around discussing her like she is a stranger? How can we be a family without her? Dad, will they call you when they need that decision?"

Claire placed her hand over Cecilia's.

"We have to let Dad decide, Cecee."

Cecilia pushed back her chair and ran from the room. Thomas stood up, but Claire stopped him with a gesture.

"No. I'll go."

Anne took Thomas's hand. How cold he was.

"Perhaps you could take me home. The girls will be calmer, when you get back, and after they've had time to process."

A few minutes later, they drove away from the stone house.

The day before, Quin waited outside Colette's hotel through the pale light of a December morning until she walked out to her car, and then he followed her to Culver's Mills. She was going to Anne's, he thought, as they passed the mill and its frozen pond. The bright blue car ahead of him slowed and parked. He circled the block and stopped where he could see her, but she wasn't likely to notice him.

Twenty minutes later, he still waited. A jogger, dressed in red and black, tapped on Colette's window. What was that all about?

Colette moved on, drifting past Catherine's home. At that moment, Anne left the house and climbed into a silver, late-model GMC truck. Adam Davidson, he thought. Where were they going? Had they found Erin?

But the two vehicles ahead of him drove to a village only five miles distant. Adam parked at the front door of a nursing home; the Chev entered the grounds but exited without stopping. He waited a few minutes, and then followed her.

He lost her somewhere in the town, and the car wasn't in the parking lot of Colette's hotel when he got there. Inside, the receptionist said that the French woman with the lovely clothes had checked out. Nothing to do but go back to Burlington, he thought.

Crossing the lobby of his hotel, he saw Colette at registration and sat behind a tall plant until she headed for the elevator. Better lucky than smart. Did she know him? He didn't think so and rode the car up with her. Fifth floor.

A few minutes later, he found her car in the outside lot beside the hotel, tagged it with a location beacon, and settled in to watch the monitor for movement.

The next morning, no car but the tag lay on the ground. She knew, he thought. She knew someone was following her. Maybe she knew him or recognized him as a man she saw in Culver's Mills. He called Thomas.

"Tom? Where are you? The Swiss woman followed Anne and the cop yesterday, but I've lost her. Where are you? Is Anne with you?"

"Goddamit, Quin. You waited until now to tell me!"

"I was behind her. Where are you?"

"I'm taking Anne back to Catherine's. The B&B?"

"Yeah. I'll meet you there."

Quin parked outside the B&B. Snow squalls, racing down the street, coating the trunks and limbs of the trees, blinded him from time to time. No lights. No movement behind the curtains of the house.

When the snow let up, he saw Tom's car parked at the curb in front of the B&B and two figures on the porch. Anne and Tom. Why did Tom hesitate before he went in? The door closed behind them, and he hurried across the street and stood on the porch. Something was wrong. No lights came on. No chatter.

He hesitated but was only a few steps away when a shot shattered one of the windows. He burst through the locked door and raced after the woman running down the hall.

Chapter Twenty-Four

Erin plodded on through the snow, one weary step in front of the other. The old snowshoes, heavier than the ones she and Adam had rented last year, dragged at her legs but held her up, out of the deep snow. It wasn't night, but the pine trees rose around her and blocked the light and with it went Erin's sense of direction. The snow tapered off to a slight whisper, and in the silence, Erin heard her footsteps. She wouldn't have known they were footsteps if they belonged to someone else, only the padding of some forest creature, a creature who wouldn't be lost, as she was, surely was. She trudged on, uphill now.

That survival course instructor. What had he said? *Seek shelter before nightfall. You can't build a shelter in the dark.* She couldn't build one in the day, with the pen-knife her only tool. Were those other forest creatures rustling the branches or Ivan? No, he wouldn't move like a breath of wind through the trees; he would race through the underbrush, scattering sleeping birds and deer. Wolves? Did wolves live in Vermont? She didn't know. Adam knew those things.

What would he do if she died in here? Who would help him? He had no family, no one to turn to. Don't, she told herself. Don't think about him. Walk, keep walking. Fatigue dragged at her legs, holding her back from her goal, the top of this little rise. Maybe there would be a road or even a highway.

Ahead, the twilight seemed brighter. A clearing? Perhaps at the edge, the shrubs would grow thick enough to be a shelter.

A cabin. A cabin. She wanted to run across to it, but was it the one she'd escaped? She hadn't looked back when she left. She didn't recognize the building, but that meant nothing. Perhaps she had walked in a circle, back to her prison and to Ivan. She couldn't stay out in the cold, in the night, alone. She put one snow-shoed foot after another, expecting him to come from the cabin at any moment, to capture her. She kept walking forward.

~

Ivan backed the van into a stump in the cabin's yard, swore, and drove down the lane. The landscape blurred with the falling snow.

A little snow, he thought. Not like in his home in Siberia, where the snow filled the roads and ploughs never came. How many years since he and Dasha fled? Now, he was alone. He pounded the steering wheel. They would pay; they would all pay. Especially that French bitch.

He wanted the egg, and he wanted to leave this country and go somewhere. They had wanted to go to Spain, to the coast where it was warm all the time. Dasha did, anyway. She loved the warmth. Long ago they had a holiday in the Crimea. The best time.

He needed the egg to flush Colette out, to kill her when she came. That's what he would do. Stalk her like a bear, and kill her.

He drove on, raging against Colette, against Dasha for being so stupid. Why did she attack someone with a gun? Always her temper. Raging against Erin, for not giving up the egg. She said she didn't have it and she gave up her friend. She told the truth. He could see it in her eyes. What would he do with her? She owed him too. She would pay when he returned to her, if he returned to her. Maybe he should leave her to rot in that cabin.

Colette. Why did she want the egg? Someone paid her. Who?

Who hired her and told her to hire him and Dasha? Who knew them?

Alexei. That KGB scum. He would say it was for Mother Russia, but Mother Russia would never see the jewels. Alexei. Not so easy to kill him.

He drove into the town, parked behind the B&B, and waited. No movement in the house. No one going in and out. Perhaps no one was home. If so, good. If not... He checked the gun in the holster under his arm, opened the van door, and sauntered across the yard to the house. No one would care.

A pane of glass stood between him and the lock. He crashed through with his elbow and entered and waited. Nothing. No screams, no footsteps. He walked across the kitchen and into a hall-way. A door opened to the left. Books, books everywhere. What was this in the corner? A safe. He squatted and looked at the lock. A gun safe. Not too hard. Before he could begin, he heard a noise from the kitchen. Someone? A cat? He crept to the hall and listened again. A figure moved between him and the light from the open door. A woman. How did she find him?

"Bonjour, Ivan."

"Cyka"

~

Adam and Pete walked the faint trail left by the van on the lane to the cabin. A few flakes of snow drifted down from the high clouds, but the storm had ended. The winter sun, shining pale through the pines overhead, cast long shadows across the road. They turned a corner and ahead, the building, its boards weathered grey, stood abandoned, or so it seemed, in a clearing. Pete took one side of the road, Adam the other and waited for long minutes. No smoke, no sign of activity. Adam motioned to Pete that he would go around to the left. Pete moved through the underbrush to the right and behind the cabin.

Still no movement. Adam startled a deer, quietly munching on cedar. She tossed an affronted white tail and disappeared into the forest. He waited. Still nothing. A broad porch stretched along the front and sides. Time to go. He crept along the floor, hugging the wall to avoid creaking the old boards. He darted his head above a window sill. Nothing inside. One door in the room. Pete came around the back and up on the porch beside him.

"Nothing in the back room. Here?"

"Nothing."

Pete tugged at the window, lifted it, and climbed through. When he reached the door, he called to Adam.

"Come around. Someone's been here. Not too long ago. Ransacked the place."

Adam stepped through and stood inside the door. Ransacked for sure. Why cut up sheets? He walked into the bedroom, saw the attic opening and called to Pete.

"Attic. I'm going to take a look."

Upstairs, he followed the tracks in the dust to the open window, but there the trail ended. If Erin had been up here, had she jumped? If she did, she walked out, unless Ivan caught her...No.

"Adam, get down here."

Pete held out a purse.

"Erin's?"

"Yes, looks like it."

He took the purse, red to match her black and red winter coat. Her identification was gone and the little Swiss knife he gave her. The scent of her perfume rose from the lining of the bag.

"It's hers. Someone jumped from the window in the attic. Did you see any signs, footprints?

"No."

"She's out there, in the snow."

Pain gripped Adam's chest, and he sank into a chair, holding the purse, smelling her scent. Why were there no prints in the snow? Where was Ivan? Pete was calling his name.

"Adam. Does she know what to do?"

"I took her on a winter survival course, but I don't know—"

"She's a smart woman. She'll survive. I'll get a search team and dogs up here."

"Okay. I'm going to walk the perimeter of the clearing."

"I'll wait for the team."

Adam stood on the porch for a moment. Which way would she go? Not out the lane.. She'd be afraid he was coming back that way. He walked away from the cabin and away from the hill behind. If she'd been thinking, that's where she would go.

He kept his eyes on the ground. Nothing. He plodded on, and then he saw, sheltered under a spreading juniper, something. Not an animal print. Not a boot or a ski. Snowshoe, maybe. North. What lay to the north but more hills? He went back to the cabin and waited.

Chapter Twenty-Five

C olette awoke to yet another snowstorm. What a country. After she found the egg and killed the McPhail, she would try somewhere warm, somewhere French in the Caribbean, for a vacation before she left for France. Better France than Switzerland. They were still looking for her in Switzerland.

Later, eating breakfast the hotel called continental—-which continent, she wondered—she exchanged glances with a black man at a nearby table. Very good looking. Yes, the Caribbean. She turned away to the view of the lake through the vast windows on one side of the room. A Christmas tree overwhelmed one corner, mirrored outside by yet another. Christmas lights everywhere in this country: hanging from the eves, outlining the balconies, ranging along the ironwork. Overdone.

When she finished, she returned to her room, dropped her gun in the pocket of her belted cashmere coat, and took the elevator to the lobby. The black man sat in a corner, reading a newspaper. He didn't look up as she passed. One more day. One more day and she would leave this place.

She'd parked her car in the furthest corner of the lot. Always she scanned for bugs and bombs before she got in a vehicle. She found the device under a door handle. What a fool. She dropped the device on the pavement. Let it keep sending.

But who was the fool? Not Ivan. Then who? Who even knew she was here? The black man? He rode up with her in the elevator last night, and now he was at breakfast. He was staying there. He paid little attention to her, except for that whole-body survey most men did. So not him.

Alexei? No, he wanted her to be successful, to find the egg for him, for Russia. A policeman? Perhaps, but not one of these small-town cops. Interpol. It must be. Cold entered her bones. Alexei on one side and Interpol on the other. What did the Americans call that? Between a rock and a hard place. Simple but true.

She must find the egg today and leave.

An hour later she drove into the lane behind the B&B and parked behind a van. What was this? Ivan, searching instead of waiting?

The back door was unlocked; she slipped through and crossed the kitchen to the hallway. Ivan stepped into the hall, saw her, whispered *bitch*, in Russian, and reached into his jacket. Too late for him. Her gun was ready. It spoke.

She clutched at the door-frame to steady herself. Another. But he would have killed her if she hadn't killed him first. He hated her for killing Dasha.

She waited for someone to respond to the sound of the shot, but nothing. Ivan's body lay across the door to a room with book-shelves. Her bullet had hit him in the chest. Blood oozed from the wound. Could he be alive? She felt for a pulse. Nothing. His eyes glared into hers. He died angry.

She searched the body. He'd been ahead of her, but he didn't find the egg. She walked into the library, saw the safe and crossed to it. Closed. Merde. Opening safes was not her best skill. Before she could attempt it, she heard voices and footsteps on the porch. McPhail. Now she would have her revenge.

~

Anne leaned back in the leather seat, breathing in the new car smell. Did they spray the aroma in, as a sort of perfume for vehicles, or did it float up from the leather on the seats, the carpeting, the hidden plastic and vinyl? The Mercedes glided away from the front of the Beauchamp home.

"A new car?"

"Mom's."

What was he thinking? That conversation with the children couldn't have been easy. How did he react to stress in his personal life? He reacted to stress in hers by taking charge, making decisions. Not collaborative. But was that a fair judgement? He'd listened to her, to the children, but he kept the decision for himself. And why was she judging him anyway? It wasn't her place, either to judge or to make the decision.

Ahead, the old mill loomed through the falling snow.

"Does seeing the old mill bother you?" he said.

She shuddered, remembering the long minutes of terror while a madman shot at her from the window in the mill, forcing her to dive under the dark water of the millpond. So many terrifying events since then. How did she feel? Shaken.

"No. Yes. Some."

"Which?"

"Some. I look to the window where he stood with the rifle."

"Next time, I'll go around the other way."

"That brings us to the back of Catherine's, where I found that poor man's body. No. It's like the courthouse. At first, the scars from the bullets that hit the wall by the front steps brought on shaking and cold, but now, nothing. The same will happen with the mill."

"And Italy."

Italy, where she was the shooter, where Esti's dead eyes stared at her, as they did most nights now.

"I hope so. I'll continue counselling with Andrea. I'm sure the anxiety will fade too. It has, some, already."

Thomas parked in front of the B&B. Anne put her hand on his arm.

"Would you like to come in for a coffee?"

"Very much."

He opened the car door for her, and they walked together up the steps to the front door. He hugged her to him.

"I can stay if you're nervous alone here," he said.

"I know, but your family needs you, too."

She turned the key in the lock and stepped inside, blinking as her eyes adjusted to the dark interior. The door closed behind her, and she switched on the light. A body lay at the foot of the stairs. Anne clutched at Thomas's right hand and turned into his coat. He shook her off.

A voice came out of the darkness of the library.

"Come in, McPhail."

Chapter Twenty-Six

Not knowing that Ivan's death abandoned her to the wilderness of snow, Erin crept up the steps of the old cabin, keeping to the outside where they shouldn't squeak. She glanced through the dirty window at the left of the door. No one. She turned the handle and swung the door out. Would he be waiting, behind the door or in the bedroom?

But she'd left a mess—jackets and boots and torn sheets and dirty dishes. This place was tidy. She crossed to the fridge. A note held by a cartoon magnet—Daffy duck with a rifle, hunting the pesky rabbit. That's how she felt, like a rabbit, but not Bugs, not a smart rabbit who got his own back, but a timid rabbit, running for her home in the ground.

Take what you need, the note read, *but leave the place as you found it.*

Yes, she would. She could do that.

A musty odour told her she shared the cabin with mice but an oil lamp, its wick trimmed and its base full of oil, promised an end to the darkness. A black wood-stove, an old-fashioned one with a reservoir for water and a white enamelled warming oven up top, stood against the outside wall to the right of the door, wood piled beside it, matches on the shelf above the burners. She opened the flue and soon had a fire burning and snow melting in a pot. The fridge was empty save for a lonely bottle of ale. She snapped the cap and took a long swallow. The freezer held a package of anonymous meat and a can of coffee. Inside a cupboard, cans of beans and corn lined up with a leftover package of corn tortillas. She heated the beans and corn and made tacos, gagging on the stale tortillas but washing them down with beer. Later, she made coffee and built up the fire. A bathroom, she thought. She would need one soon.

Through the window in the bedroom, she saw the outhouse, twenty feet or more from the door. She wouldn't be able to shovel all that way, at least until she rested. In the corner of the bedroom, a dry sink held a bowl and ewer and soap dish. Perhaps underneath? Yes. The cupboard door opened to reveal a thunder jug and toilet paper.

She turned down the lamp and snuggled under a quilt on the worn brown sofa. For what seemed like hours, she lay there, thinking of Adam and Bermuda until her fear eased and she slept.

∾

Anne gasped, her heart pounded, and her legs threatened to let her go. Who lay there? Not Catherine. Not one of her boys. Whose body was this? Who spoke from the library?

"Who did you kill?" Thomas said.

"A fool who thought he could kill me. Don't make that mistake."

Anne glimpsed the body's face. Ivan. Did this woman know where Erin was? Why had Thomas brushed her away? He must want his right hand free. What if he were armed? She trembled, bit her lip to get control and spoke.

"Who are you?"

The woman moved out into the light, a gun fitted with a silencer in her hand. Thin, dark-haired, impeccable makeup. Who wore makeup to a murder? Where had she seen her before? Evan's, she thought. She sat at the next table.

"Her name is Colette, and Interpol has searched for her for a long time. I didn't think field work was your style?"

"Because of her, I am in this godforsaken country."

Fear gripped her throat, but she pushed the words out past it.

"Me? I don't know you. What did I do?"

"She directed the action in Bermuda and Spain, and you messed up her plans," Thomas said.

Colette held her focus and the gun on Anne.

"And I will take my revenge, but first I want the egg."

"We don't have it," Thomas said.

"There is a safe. Open it."

"I don't have—" Anne said.

"Then you will die."

"Anne." Thomas's voice held a warning note. "Give her what she wants."

"I'll try. I watched Catherine."

Anne knelt in front of the safe and willed her shaking fingers to punch the numbers in the keypad. Her kids' birthdays, Catherine said. The twins had the same birthday. No, one was born at 11:50 pm and the other at 12:10 am. What was the date? She paused.

"The numbers, McPhail."

"I'm trying to remember. I am. Give me a moment."

November third and November fourth, 1999. But what order? She closed her eyes and remembered, and punched in 113499. The light on the safe clicked green.

"Move away."

Inside, Catherine's Luger lay in its holster, on top of the jewel case. Colette shoved her aside, and she fell to the carpet, her head striking the base of a torchière. Blood dribbled down her face to the floor. She pulled herself to standing and face Colette.

"A pistol. You thought you could get me first? That will not happen."

"The jewels are in the case underneath."

Colette opened the case, checked the jewellery and stuffed it in a pocket. She forced the pistol into Anne's neck at the base of her throat. Steel was cold, she thought. Always cold.

"The egg."

She forced the answer out past her fear.

"I never saw an egg."

Colette fired over Thomas's head, shattering the window behind him.

"The next will take him from you. The egg."

"Police are on their way—"

The front door crashed in. Who? Colette swivelled and bolted through the door to the kitchen. Someone thundered after her.

"Thomas, who?"

"Quin."

～

Anne collapsed on the sofa, and Thomas put his arm around her.

"I'm sorry I pushed you away—"

"She was going to kill me, us? You wanted your hand free. Are you armed? Do you carry a gun, Thomas."

"No, but I'm trained. Given a chance, I would have taken it from her."

"Or she would have killed you."

"She didn't."

What could she do? Catherine's beautiful front door, the glass shattered, the old oak splintered hung open.

"I'm going to clean up—"

"Wait until Quin comes back."

"Now the jewels that were meant to pay for Mrs. Akers' care are gone. What can we do?"

"Don't worry about her. She'll be cared for. I'm worried about you. You and Erin."

The kitchen door squeaked open.

"Thomas, what if—"

Thomas grabbed the gun from the open safe and slammed the clip in place. He pushed her down behind the sofa and stood, left hand bracing his right, aiming at the door. Quin appeared in the doorway. Thomas lowered his arm. Her heart, racing from the moment they walked through the front door, slowed and her shoulders relaxed.

"For God's sake, Tom. It's me."

"Could just as well have been her. She's a pro, too."

Thomas reached a hand to Anne and hugged her to him.

"Who's in the hallway?" Quin asked.

"Ivan, the guy who kidnapped Erin."

"Dead?"

"Gloves," he said to Quin.

How did he know Quin carried latex gloves? Did all spies? Daniel didn't. No gloves. At least none that she saw during that race across Europe to save Naomi. And all the time that woman was hating her and plotting revenge.

Thomas knelt down beside Ivan and felt his neck. He searched the pockets and handed Quin a cellphone.

"Yeah, dead."

"You?"

"He wouldn't be dead. Colette shot him. He was our only link to Erin. Check out the phone."

"Nothing much. Texts with the woman."

Quin handed him the phone, open at a text. *Call me when you have it.*

"Who's it from."

"Alexei. Likely Alexei Sokolov, former KGB and go-to guy for off-the-books. Likely the handler."

"Wouldn't he be handling the woman."

"Can't say. He might play them against each other."

"Did she control Esti and Sergio?" Anne asked from the couch.

Thomas glanced up from where he knelt by the body.

"Yes."

She closed her eyes and listened to Thomas's calm voice call the station, and speak to the police and then Quin. He replaced the gun in the safe but left the door open.

"Pete and Adam are on their way north. She said he would call Dave and he'd be here in a few minutes. You're our friend who met us here, interrupted Colette, chased her across the field and lost her."

"Sounds about right."

"What name?"

"Quin Randall."

And that was the story they gave, when Dave Graham, Pete's younger brother arrived to investigate.

Anne sat on the couch while the terse words, batted between them, flew over her. That woman escaped, and she wanted to kill her. But she wouldn't let that happen. She was stronger than that. She had to be stronger than that.

Chapter Twenty-Seven

C olette drove through the snow towards Burlington. Would he be ahead of her, or behind? She abandoned her car in an outside lot and, once in her room, packed, called a car rental place that promised delivery, and checked out with the hotel online service.

She strolled through the empty lobby and met the driver at the entrance. Once she had swept the car for bugs, she drove north-east to the skiing centre, Stowe.

She stopped at a resort that had a variety of rooms, including a motel section, far from the lobby and curious tourists. After registering under one of her names, she parked in front of her unit and carried her bags to the beige, anonymous room. A fake-impressionist painting, something in the style of Sisley overhung the bed, screwed to the wall. Why did hotels do that? Who would steal such a piece of non-art? Did people risk their freedom for a reproduction?

She wanted only to escape from this state and this country. Canada was so close. Montreal was so close. She collapsed on the bed and stared at the miniature cut-glass chandelier above her.

But Alexei would give her no peace. He insisted the egg was in Culver's Mills. Such a little town. Why? Why would it be there? She never asked Alexei how he knew and why he was so precise about where it was.

She needed sleep but she lay awake for long hours. Would the local police find her here? Not likely with so many French people in the hotel. The girl at the desk spoke to her in the dialect of Quebec.

Enough. She would do her own research. She switched on the light and padded across the room to the minibar in the corner, chose a red wine—American, but what will you— and set up her computer.

An hour, two, went by. Weak morning light crept through the crack in the drapes and fell across the keyboard. She sipped the last of the wine and saved the file in front of her. She found a memoir by a butler of the Dowager Empress Maria Feodorovna. After the revolution and the deaths of all her family, the Dowager was taken aboard a British battleship and transported to England. She carried jewels with her. Would she take some of the eggs, gifts from her husband and son, with her? Other websites suggest that she took at least one.

The Soviet army confiscated most of the fabulous jewels and they were now in the Kremlin. Had she saved one? But how would it get to Vermont, to such a small town? Perhaps it didn't exist, and she was chasing a fable.

She found a servant who left Russia with the royal entourage but stayed in Britain when the Empress moved to Denmark, where she lived until the end of her life. She could follow the genealogy of the servant, or she could find out who McPhail visited in the retirement home. Perhaps that.

And that kidnapped woman. She would know where the egg was, but that stupid Ivan told no one where he had hidden her. If the police found her, if she came back to Culver's Mills perhaps it would be possible to get the information from her.

But what of McPhail. It would be quicker to follow her, to get her alone and force the knowledge from her. And then she would kill her. Unbidden, the image of Ivan's angry face rose in front of her. She opened the second bottle of wine.

~

The apparatus of investigation followed Dave Graham—testing the body, marking off the scene with yellow tape. Under the careful eye of a young deputy, Anne gathered her belongings and came back downstairs. Dave and Thomas were talking.

"What did she get away with?" Dave said.

"Erin's jewels. She asked Catherine to keep them in her safe after the break-in," Anne said.

"Who was she?"

"I don't know. French, I think. Elegant."

"Elegant?"

"I saw her at Evan's a few days ago."

"Fingerprints?" he asked Thomas.

"Gloves."

Dave stepped out of the room, talking into his phone.

"Is Jamieson still the chief here?" she asked.

"Yes. Why?"

"I wondered if Dave needed a little help."

"He'll call Pete."

While the investigation went on around them, they sat together on the sofa. Thomas held her against him for long moments until the trembling stopped. His familiar scent, a mixture of soap and something else, his lemony shaving cream perhaps, comforted her but then she remembered Erin.

"What about Erin? Was there anything his pockets to show where he kept her?"

"No, but Adam and Pete have a lead and are on their way up north to the mountains. Someone reported renting a cabin to him."

"Dave told you?"

"He played ball with Daniel."

Small towns, she thought. It was too small a town to hide in but Colette was trained. She could disappear in Burlington and wait, a spider at the centre of a web.

"She's still out there and she wants to kill me."

Anne struggled off the couch and paced the room. Thomas leaned back and watched her quick march in the small space.

"I won't let her. We'll find her, Annie. We will."

She sat down again and grasped his arm. His muscles tensed under the sleeve of his jacket, the fabric rough on her fingers.

"What if I left?"

He shifted then, to search her face with his eyes, and put one gentle hand around her head tangling his fingers in her soft blonde curls.

"She would follow you because you can be sure she knows all about you. Her speciality is information."

Information. She would never be safe from Colette.

"Couldn't Brad locate where the phone has been?"

"The area, maybe. Are you coming home with me?"

He had to go home, to his family.

"No, maybe. I have to clean up here and call someone to fix the window. I could go to a hotel."

"Catherine may have plywood that I can use to cover the window and door. I'll make a call to a guy who'll come out to fix it in the morning. But you can't stay alone. She still has her mission and if she was angry with you before—"

"I don't know what to do, Thomas. I don't want to be foolish but your family—"

"It's Christmas morning. I have to go out to the house. My grandchildren—"

"Oh, Thomas, I'm sorry. I'd forgotten the day. Of course, I'll come."

"After I do something about that window."

~

Colette walked across the terrazzo floor of the retirement home to the antique mahogany desk. A grey-haired woman beamed at her.

"I would like to visit one of your guests," Colette said.

"Oh, certainly. Our people all enjoy the company. Perhaps you would like to stay for our Christmas lunch that is starting in a few minutes. You can choose from a menu before you go up to see her."

"No. I don't want to bother her if she is fatigued from my cousin Anne's visit yesterday."

"Oh, are you Doctor McPhail's cousin? She's a lovely woman. No, Mrs. Akers was quite happy to talk to her and that nice policeman. Well, I guess he's not a policeman anymore. So sad about his fiancée. Did you know her?"

Colette interrupted the flow of speech.

"Could I see Mrs. Akers now?"

"Oh, of course, dear. Room 105, down the hall to your right. I would take you, but we're expecting guests for lunch."

"I can find my way, thank you."

Colette knocked at the door and opened it at the cheerful call to come in.

A smile lit up the face of a white-haired woman sitting in the bow window of the room. Beyond her, the snow-covered lawn faded into a stand of trees and shrubs.

"Hello," she said. "Merry Christmas. Who are you?"

"Merry Christmas. I am Marianne. Anne McPhail sent me to ask you some more questions about the Russian objects."

The elderly woman waved her hand towards an armchair across from hers.

"Come in and sit down for a few minutes but Christmas lunch will be starting shortly."

The old woman's face, open and friendly had a foolish look. She would be easy to get information from, Colette thought.

"Do you remember anything more about the location of the egg and jewels?"

Mrs. Akers frowned and leaned forward to tap Colette's knee.

"I'm afraid not. In fact, it was news to me that there was an egg involved. I never saw one, and my mother said nothing about an imperial egg."

"Nothing."

"No."

"Is there anyone else we could ask?"

"No. I'm the last. The secret went with my great-grandmother to her grave."

"Merde."

"Now that is not at all a nice thing to say."

"My apologies. I have been hunting a long time."

"Indeed."

The dinner bell rang, and an aide came to the door to help Mrs. Akers with her walker.

"Goodbye," she said,

Colette rushed from the room and out to her car. Nothing. If the old woman was telling the truth? And, why wouldn't she? She believed her story; she believed that she was McPhail's cousin.

In the dining room, Mrs. Akers tapped her finger on the white tablecloth.

"Emily?" her friend asked. "Where are you?"

"I was thinking that younger people believe we are so credulous. A woman who was here before lunch told me a pack of lies to get information from me."

"And?"

"She didn't. But now that I see the opposition, I may call the doctor and her charming friend who came to see me yesterday. Yes, I might do that."

She picked up her fork. She had kept a detail from Anne. She would call her after her nap.

Chapter Twenty-Eight

The door and window repaired enough to withstand the weather and statements given at the station, Thomas and Anne drove out to his home. A wreath of green fir branches, dotted with silver bells, decorated the front door. A uniformed maid hustled along the hall to relieve them of their coats and boots. Somewhere, Christmas carols played.

"Where is everyone?" Thomas asked.

"In the conservatory."

The conservatory, an elegant glass and steel Victorian structure, wreathed in flowering plants, overlooked the winter garden. Monkish figures—the evergreens bundled in wraps—dotted the landscape. Low bushes, still laden with summer berries—food for the birds—outlined the terrace. Cardinals and blue jays, flying in and out of the shrubs, outshone the American goldfinches in their drab winter feathers.

The adults in the family lounged on white wicker and wrought-iron chairs and on a sofa, cheerful in a chintz cover, watching over the three children. Daniel's son Tommy, now almost four years old and Claire's twin girls, just past two, played in the centre of the carpet with a heap of Christmas toys. Tommy drove a red train engine up and over a track that crossed the room and back again. The music, louder here, came from built-in speakers.

"Grandpa."

The children swarmed Thomas, and he dragged a girl on each leg with Tommy holding his hand, over to an armchair. Anne sank into a chair near the door. Daniel noticed her first. He patted the space beside him on the sofa.

"Anne, come sit over here."

She caught a glance between Cecilia and Claire. Would it start all over again? She wouldn't stay if it did but would get on a plane and fly home.

"Anne, would you like a mimosa? We're toasting the day," Cecilia said.

"Have you eaten?" Claire said.

"I'd love a mimosa. No, we haven't eaten. It's been quite some twenty-four hours."

"Dad?"

"Scotch. I'll tell you what went on later. Did the kids open all their presents?"

"Yes, we didn't have the heart to stop them, with Grandmama and you and Anne not here."

What was this, Anne wondered. Had they made a pact amongst them to treat her well or was it a temporary lull until Christmas was over? She took her sparkling, yellow drink from Cecilia. Beautiful crystal, she thought. Waterford.

"They called from the hospital, Dad," said Claire. "Grandmama is slipping, whatever that means and they think we should visit today. Should we all go?"

"I'll stay with the kids," said Daniel's wife.

"Yes, we should all go. Will you come?" he said, turning to Anne.

"Unless you'd rather I didn't."

Anne caught that glance between the girls again.

"No, we want you with us," said Claire.

After their drinks and some food, they divided into two groups and arranged to meet at the hospital. Daniel drove his sisters in the SUV and Anne and Thomas left in the sedan.

"What was that?" she asked.

"That's what the girls do. If they decide on a course of action, they carry through together."

"I caught a couple of glances between them. Is one more welcoming than the other?"

"I don't think so. The girls have always done that. A twin thing, they call it."

"I hope so."

Thomas ran his hand over her hair and then put the car in gear.

～

His family ahead of him, Thomas drove away from the home he shared with his mother. Had he seen her there, sitting at the head of the mahogany table, kneeling in her rose garden, or patiently pulling weeds and adding them to the basket at her feet, for the last time? He couldn't have raised the children without her, her kindness, her strength.

The woman who sat beside him now, her hands folded in her lap, had the same strength and compassion. But she didn't want to live in Vermont. She loved her city and her stone house by the lake. Her own country, too. Her feelings about the political direction America was taking were vehement and negative. Could they make it work, for both of them, for the children? If Anne thought she was coming between him and the children, she would leave. She was firm on that.

Anne touched his arm.

"I'm here," she said.

"I want to make it work."

"So do I and we will. But first, we have to get through all of this —your mother, the children, Erin, that woman."

"I'll keep you safe. I promise."

He took her hand and held it until they entered Burlington and turned at the gate to the hospital. Neither of them noticed the car that followed at a distance.

They met the others at the doors of the hospital, and a few minutes later, he left them alone in the waiting room. He opened the door to the intensive care, aware of the silence beneath the whisper of the ventilators and the murmurs of the nurses at the desk, and walked through to his mother's room. She was so still, he thought, so bird-like. Her blue-veined hands lay on the bedcover, a little darker than the white sheets but not by much. He held one. So cold, as though her heart didn't have the strength to pump warm blood that far. Her face drooped, and her eyes were closed.

"Mom?"

No response unless one eyelid flickered. A voice spoke to him.

"Mister Beauchamp?"

A tall, fair-haired woman, concern in her eyes stood at the entrance to the room.

"Yes."

"I'm Andrea, your mother's nurse. The doctor wanted me to call him when you arrived. Is that okay?"

"Yes, of course. Has Mom woken at all?"

"No, not today."

"Does the doctor know how long?"

"I don't think so."

He stroked his mother's hand again, told her how much she meant to him and whispered that he loved her.

Later, he walked out toward his waiting family.

∼

Colette parked around the corner from the B&B, with a view of the street and the house. An hour, two went by. She called Alexei.

"I have the jewellery, but not the egg."

"Not good enough, Colette. I don't care about the jewellery. You can keep it for yourself if you find the egg. But if you don't, the jewellery won't be all you will lose."

"I have to get McPhail alone, and I will—"

"Do it. Twenty-four hours, Colette."

She rested her head against the back of her seat and closed her eyes. Twenty-four hours. She opened her eyes at the sound of a car's engine. She slouched in her seat until they drove past. Who was the man? Someone had helped McPhail in Spain. Was it he? She followed at a discreet distance until the car ahead turned in to an estate. No security at the gate. She noted the number, drove on, and parked.

Her databases gave her the name of the owner—Thomas Beauchamp—and some information: wealthy American business-man, no affiliation with law enforcement or intelligence. Nothing was known, but someone got her out of Spain; someone cleaned up. Esti disappeared, killed or paid off. A smooth operation. She suspected Mossad but could never be sure. She waited near the gates. Estates, not houses here, she thought. Must take a great deal of money to keep them up.

She switched data on and began searching her databases again. Beauchamp was a wealthy man; he would pay to get her back, but kidnapping was a dirty business. Better to kill her and put a clean end to it.

Another hour of waiting before two vehicles left the driveway, three people in an SUV first and then the car that she had followed from the B&B. She would tag that one and when he left her alone, take her.

Sitting at the narrow desk in the anonymous room, holding his phone with one hand and writing with the other, Quin noted the town and hotel his contact had given him.

"Thanks, buddy. I owe you."

The name the woman had used on the register was one of

Colette's known aliases. Known to that guy in Spain who had helped them try to take her down. He set his GPS with the address for the motel.

An hour later, he parked outside the one-story white building that housed the office for the resort. A wing stretched off to the right with cars parked in front of most of the units. One spot was vacant. He walked up to the desk to speak to the teenaged girl standing behind it.

"Do you have any free units in the motel section?"

"I'm so sorry, but we are booked solid."

"There's no car at number seven."

"I'll look. No, Madame Desbarets is still with us."

With that, her hand flew to her mouth.

"I shouldn't tell—-"

"Already forgotten. Don't worry about it."

He drove off, parked in the lot for the resort, and waited. Half-an-hour later, the teenager walked away, her backpack swinging from one shoulder. He strolled past the office where an older woman took the position behind the desk. At unit seven, he paused, checked for watchers, worked the lock for a moment, and stepped inside.

He searched the room and her bags. Too much luggage for a working spy, he thought. But then, as far as they knew, she hadn't much field experience, which explained the trail of dead bodies she was leaving. Buried in one bag, beneath a neatly-folded stack of colourful scarves, he found the jewellery taken from Catherine's safe. He pocketed it and moved on. Nothing else. Why did she leave the jewels behind in such a vulnerable place? Unless they weren't all that she was after. Whoever handled her must want the egg, and she wanted revenge. He returned the room to its usual state and slipped out.

Back in his car, he called Thomas.

"Tom, I found the jewels, but she's not here. Watch Anne."

"She's with me. Thanks. Are you coming back to Culver's?"

"I'll return the jewels to Erin when they find her. So, yeah, eventually. I'm staying here for a few hours."

"They're tracking Erin with the dogs. She escaped from where Ivan was holding her, but it's a big mountain."

"Yes, it is. Are you with your family?"

"Yes."

"Happy Christmas."

In the waiting room for intensive care, Daniel leaned forward in his chair, focussed on the geometric pattern in the grey and tan rug that defined their family's space.

"How do you think she is?" he said.

Claire and Cecilia, side by side on a long sofa, their blonde heads tilted just a fraction, Claire's to the right, Cecilia's to the left.

"Better," Claire said. "I think she'll be better. Some people recover from strokes, almost back to normal."

"Why did they ask us if we were coming over?"

"Because it's Christmas," said Cecilia. "Because it's Christmas, after all."

"What do you think, Anne?"

Why? Why would they call the family except they thought she was going. She wouldn't say that. Families never forgot who gave them bad news about a beloved person. Sometimes they changed doctors because of it. She wouldn't say anything, no opinion.

"I think we should wait for Thomas."

"That means you're pessimistic," Claire said.

"No. I don't have enough information to be pessimistic or otherwise. Waiting is the hardest part for the family of someone who is ill. Hospitals move in their own rhythms, and they are never fast enough."

"Why? Why don't they care? Why doesn't Dad come out? He's been ages." Cecilia said.

"Fifteen minutes," said Daniel. "He's only been fifteen minutes."

"I'm going in."

"No." Daniel and Claire said in unison.

"Dad said to wait. What if he's in conference with the doctors?"

They tossed it back and forth. Thomas had a strong hand in the family, Anne thought. Would she have done it differently, more inclusively? Maybe. But she had no personal experience with making this sort of decision or with this family. Her parents were alive and well and living close to her aunts in Victoria, B.C. When the time came, how would she and her sister, and her sister's children and all the nieces and nephews interact? It would be up to her; her parents had told her when they sent the copies of their living wills. She was their attorney for personal care, but everyone would want a say, especially Liz.

"Anne?" Daniel said.

"Yes."

"Should one of us go in, or should you?"

"No, certainly not me and I think you should wait."

Cecelia stood up.

"Cecee?" Claire said.

"I have to move."

She walked the length of the waiting room and stood at the windows but swivelled back when the door to the room opened.

Thomas walked to the family and held his hand out to Cecilia when she got to him.

"Grandmama is still with us, but slipping away. The doctor doesn't know how long."

He sat on the sofa beside his girls, one on either side. His red-rimmed eyes met Anne's for a moment. What a loss for him, she thought. She was not only his mother but the woman who helped him raise his children, who made his home and was always there when he returned.

"Can we see her?" Daniel asked.

"Yes, two at a time. Why don't you go in with Cecee first?"

Daniel and Cecilia disappeared behind the door to their grandmother's room. Claire took her father's hand and put her head on his shoulder.

"What will we do without her, Dad."

"Go on, sweetheart. Go on."

They waited.

~

Colette strolled down the lanes in the outside parking. She was sure they hadn't gone underground. When she spotted the car, she sidled between it and a green Chevrolet. She dropped her bag, leaned forward to pick it up and at that moment tucked a tracking beacon inside the bumper of Thomas's car. She moved away and ambled on towards her car at the end of the lot.

She opened her laptop and accessed the program that traced the car's movements. The tracker emitted a gentle ping every fifteen seconds and displayed it on a map. Now she could proceed with the rest of her plan, to retrieve the jewellery and make her escape to Canada as soon as she found the egg.

Her phone played its melody, the opening bars of The Steppes of Central Asia. Alexei.

"The egg?"

"Not yet. I'm tracking McPhail. I talked to the woman who inherited the jewels from her ancestor, a servant of Maria Feodorovna. The family knows nothing about the egg."

"Do you believe her?"

"A foolish old woman. Yes, I believe her."

"Someone lied, the woman or the ancestor. The egg is there, somewhere."

"The ancestor. The woman knew very little."

"You think this McPhail knows where it is?"

"Or she can find it."

"Either way, this has gone on too long. Find the egg and bring it to me, or I will find you."

"Don't threaten me, Alexei."

"Remember you work for me, or your child will pay the price."

Her chest tightened, and she forgot to breathe. How had Alexei found out about her child? No one knew. No one. Perhaps they knew she had a child but didn't know where she was. How could they know? She was never careless, never visited, never texted or emailed. If she called, it was from an anonymous phone. And the nuns would not give information to anyone. But Monique was eleven years old now. Perhaps she told someone something, enough to betray the secret.

"I'll find the egg."

"I'll be waiting."

Fear gripped her heart, and the pain bent her double over the steering wheel. How had he found her daughter? She took a burner cell phone from its hiding place inside the lining of the door. Only one number programmed in.

"Ma Mere? It is I, Colette."

"Yes?"

"It is time to move her."

"I will take her into the cloister for retreat. Call me when she may return to us."

Colette clicked off her phone, took out the sim card and smashed it and dumped the phone's carcass by the side of the road.

In Switzerland, a nun, in modern-day dress of beige skirt, white blouse, and navy sweater, a crucifix hanging from a silver chain around her neck, touched the intercom.

"Sister, bring Monique to me."

An hour later, Monique, dazed by the sudden move, sat in a limousine bearing her away from the school. A few miles distant they entered the gates of another convent, this one surrounded by a high wall. Only one dark oak door, other than the formidable iron that barred the way in for cars, pierced the facade. The sister spoke into the intercom, the grate opened, and one eye peered at her. The bolts inside protested as they were drawn and then the door opened.

They crossed the threshold and disappeared into the ancient stone building. The door closed behind the woman and the child. Safe. Safe for now, the nun thought.

Chapter Twenty-Nine

Christmas was in Adam's thoughts. They had planned a day with each other in the loft—opening presents, going for a walk in the snow, eating a simple dinner in front of the fire—but instead, she was alone, somewhere in that wilderness of white. He dozed and woke, dozed again.

"Adam."

Adam stirred and bolted upright.

"What?"

"Sorry, but the dogs are here."

They met the searchers and the two bloodhounds and one beagle that came with them. The search team off-loaded a pair of snowmobiles, snowshoes and skis.

"Morning," Pete said. "Thanks for coming out."

"Yup," said one handler.

The other searcher handed Pete a thermos.

"Coffee."

They nodded their thanks and Pete went back in for mugs.

"A beagle?" said Adam.

"Best of the bunch," said the man on the other end of the leash. "What do you have that she handled?"

After the dogs had a good sniff of Erin's purse, the beagle ran in excited circles around the cabin, stopping at the bush where Adam had found the snowshoe print. His handler snapped him back on the lead, and the other two took up positions a distance from him and plunged into the forest.

Adam and Pete rode with the snowmobiles behind the dogs. Up above, a helicopter circled, looking for signs of human activity below.

The deep snow clogged the runners of the machines, and they stopped from time to time to clear them. Far ahead, the excited yips of the beagle and the baying from the bloodhounds suggested that they, at least, sensed they had a trail to follow.

Adam stood up, brushing the snow from his jacket.

"We're not much good back here," he said.

"The team didn't want us confusing the dogs."

Adam pointed toward the sound of the helicopter.

"What about the eyes up above?"

"Nothing so far."

"Do you have a map?"

Pete handed Adam a topographical map of the mountain. He followed the highway north to where it ended at Richford.

"If she kept on going straight, she'd come out near the border."

"Or across it."

"They'd stop her."

"If they saw her. She wouldn't even know she crossed."

"What if we went to Richford and came back this way?"

"We could try, but it's a big mountain."

Pete talked to the search team, and they went back to the truck and drove to the highway and turned north. The team with the dogs slogged on through the forest.

Erin stretched her arms and her cramped legs and hoisted herself to sitting. How long had she slept? She crept over to a window. Outside, the snow fell again, and dark clouds pressed on the hilltops. She'd have to go soon, while the snow would still obliterate her footsteps. She would walk on towards what she thought was north.

She boiled down snow on the woodstove and mixed instant coffee with the boiling water to make a potent brew. She'd saved a taco from the night before and forced the dry tortilla down her unwilling throat. Later, after she dressed for outside, she carried the thunder jug from the bedroom to the outhouse. The door was frozen shut and drifts piled half-way up the front. Walking further back into the woods, she dumped the contents and took the jug back to the cabin, washed it out with the remains of the water and returned it to its place in the cabinet. Time to go. She looked back when she reached the woods on the north side of the clearing. No smoke rose from the chimney. If the snow kept up, he wouldn't find her.

After a few metres, she stopped at a trail that a snowmobilers' association had cut through the forest. She walked a short way towards what she thought was west. A signpost told her the distance to the lakes. It must be going west. The I89 ran north and south but took a curve to the west. Was there a smaller highway? She tried to remember the map for that part of the state. At that moment, her foot hit a buried rock or log and she tumbled down a slope, her arms flailing out to grab at bushes and trees, her snow-shoes catching on errant branches until she reached the bottom. Bone-deep pain shot from her wrist to her shoulder.

"Damn. Oh, damn."

Her voice startled a chickadee from a nearby shrub, sending it up in a tiny flurry of snow and annoyed chirps.

What had she done? Was her arm broken? How would she climb back up that slope? She tried to pull herself up, but the pain dropped her to the ground, and she lay still until cold crept in and urged her to stand. She struggled to sit upright, took off the snow-shoes and used one of them as a crutch. She leaned against a nearby tree and strapped them on again. Too loose, but maybe they would stay on long enough to get her to the top.

Or did she have to go up? She had hurtled down the north side of the trail. She could walk towards the west. Maybe the hill wouldn't be so steep further on. Her arm was broken at the wrist, her hand flailing uselessly. She tucked her arm inside her shirt to form a sling and buttoned her coat around it. The effort exhausted her.

"Shall I stay here, tree, sitting against you until they come for me."

Her voice shattered the quiet and drove a protesting finch from the bush beside her.

But they would never find her. She had to walk. One foot ahead of the other, towards the west.

Chapter Thirty

At the hospital, Anne made coffee in an alcove off the waiting room that was fitted with a kettle and a Keurig. She carried the cups back to Thomas and Claire and returned for her own. No machine coffee here. A small thing, she thought, but it made a difference, made the waiting a tiny bit easier.

"Do you want to go in with me, Anne?" Claire asked.

"No, I'll stay here with Thomas."

Cecilia and Daniel walked past the nurses' station towards them. Cecelia sat again on the green sofa beside Claire.

"She's not there anymore," Cecilia said to her twin.

They held each other and cried. Daniel slumped in an armchair and closed his eyes.

Waiting was worse, Anne thought, worse than a sudden death for those left behind. But waiting while someone you loved dwindled away was so difficult. She remembered the long days with Michael and the last few hours when he lay in her arms and then he was gone. So long ago now, but the pain, in this setting, watching other people's grief, brought it back. She wiped away a tear and reached for Thomas's hand.

"Anne?"

"Thinking of other losses."

"Me, too."

Claire walked over to her brother.

"Shall we go in, Daniel."

Daniel had his arm around her shoulder when they disappeared into the room. A moment later, a thin man in a white coat bustled along the corridor and opened the same door.

"Grandmama's doctor," Cecilia said.

"Perhaps they called him to speak to Thomas."

"Perhaps."

Death in the family changes everything, changes relationships, drawing some closer, putting a deep gulf between others. But perhaps the old lady wouldn't die, at least not yet, but would linger, a ghost of herself. That, too, increased the stress on the family, on relationships. What would either outcome do to her and Thomas?

She closed her eyes and waited. When the white-coated doctor said Thomas's name, she sat upright.

"Doctor Patton, you've met my friend Doctor McPhail."

"Yes. Could I speak to the family, Thomas? Daniel and Claire will be right out."

His face, grave but sympathetic, glanced at her.

"Anne will be with us."

"Of course."

The others came out, and the family followed him to a conference room next to the nursing station.

"I'm sure you have questions, and I'll answer them, but first, I should tell you that your grandmother isn't suffering any pain as far as we can tell. She's not responsive—"

"Will she be?" said Claire.

"Perhaps, although with each passing day it becomes less likely."

Cecilia thumped her hands on the oak conference table.

"Why can't you be sure? I feel like we're on a death watch or at a wake. The nurse said talk to her, be cheerful, play music. How can we when you say she is almost dead?"

"Cecee," Thomas said.

"I know, Dad. I'm behaving badly. I don't know what to do."

Anne got up and walked around the table to Cecilia, sat beside her and put her arm around her.

"We have to behave as though she is with us. It's part of recovery," the doctor said.

He went on to explain what they would do, and again what a DNR meant. Finally, he asked what steps they would like to take in the new year.

"We can move her to our palliative care area, or you can take her home. I would only suggest home if someone in the family were there to supervise the care."

"We'll discuss it, and I'll call you," said Thomas. "May we have this room for a while?"

"Take all the time you need."

He left, leaving silence and grief behind. Anne took her arm from around Cecilia's shoulders and spoke to Thomas, "Could I suggest something."

"Of course," said Thomas.

"I think it would be best to go home, process what you learned from the doctor. It takes time and that time shouldn't be spent here unless one or more of you want to stay with her."

"I want to stay, for a while," said Cecilia, "but I'd like to be home when you talk about it."

"We'll leave you the car, and I'll call you," said Thomas.

A short time later, they left. Anne watched from the elevator as Cecilia straightened her shoulders and pushed open the door to her grandmother's room. No DNR. If the possibility arose, would Cecilia intervene and force a resuscitation? Had that occurred to Thomas? She should talk to him, but not until later, until they were home.

Colette waited, reading a book in a cafe close to the hospital, drawing curious glances from the students who were the usual clientele. Her phone, nestled in her lap, pinged every few minutes, a quiet reminder that the car she waited for hadn't left the parking lot.

Two hours late, a series of rapid-fire sounds alerted her that the car was moving. She bundled her book and phone into her bag and hurried out the door to where her car waited at the curb.

The sedan was ahead of her about two kilometres when it took the highway north, and she wanted to close that gap.

A few flakes of snow fell, and then a steady stream in her headlights, slanted by the wind. When she got closer, she saw one woman in the car, bundled in a parka, peering at the road ahead.

The road curved up and around a pine-covered hill. The drop on one side looked a satisfying ten metres. Would the woman survive that? It didn't matter. She would stop and finish her.

She drove up to the sedan and hit the back with a satisfying wail from the bumper. The car ahead wavered and spun, ending up facing her, before the woman behind the wheel fought for control and, winning it, accelerated past her and back towards Burlington.

Who was that? The face that stared into hers was not McPhail. It was no one she knew, and soon the police would have a description of her. She drew into a rest-stop by the highway and called up a list of motels on the GPS.

On the north side of Culver's Mills, she followed the GPS to a narrow street. Warehouses and a factory loomed on either side. Who would build a motel in an industrial zone? Where was this irritating voice in the computer taking her? Then she saw it, a red-tiled roof visible among the grey buildings. No cars in front. Good. No one to see her arrive but whoever was behind the counter. Only six units, three up and three down. Outside corridor. Why outside, in this frigid country? She parked in front of the office, an addition to one end.

Inside, the smell of curry, garlic, and, above it all, tobacco smoke almost drove her out again. A tiny woman, her face a mass of wrinkles, came out wiping her hands on a yellow-banded glass cloth. Indian or Pakistani, Colette thought.

"Do you have a free unit on the ground level?"

The old woman looked her up and down.

"For you?"

"Yes. Who else?"

"Fifty dollars."

"A hundred if you forget I am here. My husband—"

"A hundred. Number three, at the end. The register?"

"I'm not here."

Colette took the key, re-parked her car in front of number three and opened the door of the unit. The smell of bleach overwhelmed the underlying aroma of too much fast food and too many bodies and their cigarettes and liquor. Someone, perhaps the old woman, had cleaned the toilet and sink. She found a spare blanket on a shelf in the closet and spread it over the bed. She wouldn't be sleeping in those sheets. A wooden chair stood in front of a scarred pine desk against the window. She sat and opened her laptop. The dot on a map told her that the car was at an address in Burlington. The police station. She would wait at that B&B. McPhail would go back there, sometime. She placed a call to France.

Chapter Thirty-One

Ahead, a white clapboard building with a high-roofed drive-through for trucks tacked on one side, marked the border at Richford/East Pinnacle. A similar structure, signed Douane, a few metres north, welcomed visitors to Canada and the Province du Quebec.

Adam pushed open a side door.

"Hey," said a guard, his hand on his sidearm.

Pete had his identification in his hand and held it out, far from his body.

"Pete Graham, Culver's Mills police."

"What can we do for you? Who's this?"

"Adam Davidson. He was Culver's Mills police. His fiancée was kidnapped, escaped, and is walking off the mountain."

"Walking?"

"Snowshoes, we think."

"Why come here? Walk through the whole village to here?"

"She's likely afraid the guy is looking for her."

"Is he?"

"Dead."

"We'll watch for her."

Adam showed them Erin's picture, gave them his phone number and left with Pete.

"What now?" Pete said.

"Coffee in the village where we can see the road, in case. Then drive back along it towards where the dogs are."

They sat in the window of a bistro in a red-brick building over-looking River Street. Adam faced east. She would walk west, he thought, if she walked along here. He knew that it was a faint hope that she would walk off the mountain. They would have to count on the dogs. He shook his head no at the waiter who hovered with a coffee pot.

"Check with the search and rescue?"

"Will do."

Pete sent a text and a few moments later, showed the reply to Adam.

Found cabin where we think she sheltered for the night, still following northwest.

"She's coming this way?"

"So far. What now?"

"Drive south. Pray."

"We'll find her. The dogs are good dogs."

"I know. But how long..."

They left the bistro and drove south, across the bridge. The black river beneath, its surface free of ice, ran high and fast.

Pete's phone buzzed.

"I'll be there. An hour or less," he said and disconnected.

"What?" said Adam.

"A body at Catherine's. Inside. Ivan, they think. Some woman shot him. Anne and Thomas are there."

"I'll wait here."

Adam swung out of the truck and crossed the bridge to the bistro. Pete took the road to Culver's Mills.

～

Ninety minutes later, after a long drive in the heavy snow, Anne and Thomas, Claire and Daniel handed their coats to the maid in the foyer of the elegant home and walked in silence in the conservatory.

"Did Cecilia text you, Dad?" asked Daniel.

"Not yet."

"She texted me she was leaving a half-hour ago," said Claire.

They sat around the room, starting conversations that sputtered to a halt after an exchange or two. What were they all waiting for, Anne wondered. Were they waiting for Cecilia to return, with her anger or for the hospital to call with news of yet another decline or for the dreary season to be over?

And what about Erin? Anne hadn't heard from Adam for hours. His last text said they were going to the border, to wait at the end of what they hoped would be Erin's long snowshoe out of the hills.

The house phone rang, but no one rushed to pick it up, glancing at each other with frightened faces, waiting for the maid to come.

"Mr. Thomas, Miss Cecilia is on the phone."

Thomas took the call. He passed his hand over his face and closed his eyes before he said, "I'll come for you, Cecee."

"Dad?"

"She's all right, Claire. Someone forced her off the road."

Daniel bounded to his feet.

"What? Where is she? I'll get her."

"No, the police want to talk to me. She was driving my car."

Anne's throat tightened, and she put her arm on Thomas's sleeve.

"She drove the car we went in. That woman is still after me."

"What woman," said Claire. "Why is someone after you?"

"Later, Claire."

"No, Dad. Who are you, Anne, that people are after you, trying to kill you?"

Her voice trembling, Anne said, "A woman——"

"Not just Anne, but me, too," said Thomas. "I'll explain later, but now I have to go to Cecee."

"I'm coming," said Anne.

"You'll be safer—"

"No."

A few minutes later, they drove away from the house, into the storm.

"I have to go home, Thomas. I can't stay here, putting everyone in danger, putting you in danger."

"Let's see what happened. Maybe it was some drunk kid, liquored-up for Christmas."

"You don't think that."

"I don't think anything. I have no facts."

"If it were Colette—"

"If it were, we'll tell the state troopers and set them on her trail. She won't hang around."

"Revenge, you said. She wants revenge."

◈

Maddy stopped texting and spoke to her grandfather.

"Grandpa, Nick and I are going out on the sleds."

Will looked up from the farmer's newspaper he read every week.

"Stay away from the cabins."

Maddy moved over to perch on the side of her grandfather's chair.

"Nick says cops are everywhere, with dogs, so we won't, but we might cross the border for a few hours."

He looked at her over the top of his reading glasses.

"Where?"

"At Richford."

"Why?"

"There's a cafe in a village we like."

He stood up and strode over to the window, waved at Nick and turned to her.

"I don't much like you crossing the border."

"Grandpa, it's Canada."

"Not America, is it?"

"No, but that's why we like to go. It's like going to Europe."

"Better Canada than Europe. It might snow again. Back before dark, and tell that young fella to behave."

"I will."

She zipped her suit up and swung on her snowmobile. Nick looked over at her and grinned.

"What did he say?"

"He said to tell you to behave yourself."

"I will."

"Let's cut to the trails north of our hunting cabins and watch for that woman they're looking for."

"Okay."

With that, Maddy buckled on her helmet, and they roared away down the lane and north towards Canada.

Thomas parked in the lot outside the low brick building, extended by a white frame addition, that was the State Police Barracks. Anne knew that the State Police had a similar organization to the military. She wondered if the extension was a barracks with the troopers living there as the Gardia did in Spain. A question for another day. Thomas walked over to the sedan, squatted down by the back bumper, and checked the scrape on the paint.

"Blue, I think."

Inside, Cecilia sat on a hardback chair, her head downcast, her eyes on her hands folded in her lap. Anne lingered by the reception desk while Thomas went to her. These places were all much the same, she thought. Grey and institutional, although a violet, blooming with tiny pink flowers, added a hint of personality to the counter. The woman behind the desk spoke to her.

"You don't want to talk to your daughter?"

"She's not my daughter, and she needs her dad."

The woman turned her attention to her computer screen. A few moments later, Thomas came over.

"May I take my daughter and my car home?" he asked.

"I'll check."

"Is she—"

Thomas shook his head, and Anne lapsed into silence.

"You can take her but could you leave the car until the day after tomorrow for processing?"

"Of course."

Thomas handed her his card and beckoned to Cecilia.

Once in the car, Thomas said, "You saw her face?"

"Yes. She looked surprised."

"Surprised? That you still had control of the car?"

"I don't know. Just surprised. Why would she do that?"

"What did she look like?" Anne asked.

"Thin, darker hair. No glasses. Her mouth was wide open like her jaw had dropped or something. Surprised. Like I was not supposed to have made it or like I was the wrong person. Who did she think I was?"

"We'll talk about it at home."

"Dad."

"No, Cecee. At home."

∾

Erin struggled up a low rise to reach the snowmobile trail she'd followed for the last hour or so. When she made the top, she stood for a moment, catching glimpses of sunshine through the trees. What time was it? She had no idea. Ahead of her another signpost at a crossing trail. This one pointed the way to Richford and Canada. Five miles. Could it be only five miles? The other sign said The Lakes. Richford sounded better, closer and a border crossing meant officials, someone who would help her, who would call Adam, and then he would come for her.

An hour later, she emerged from the trees into a meadow, high on the side of the mountain. What mountain was it? She wanted to run, to take off the heavy snowshoes and race across the vast space and down to the valley. The town, some town, some houses must be down there. *Never abandon equipment unless you're forced to.* Did Adam say that or the instructor at that survival course? She swung her foot forward.

Half-way across the meadow, engines coming up behind her slowed. Her heart felt as though it stopped. Was it Ivan? She'd come so far. How would he get a snow machine?

But the concerned face that looked at her from the helmet wasn't Ivan but dark-haired young girl with a wash of freckles across her upturned nose. Erin took a breath and her good arm, fisted, relaxed.

"Hi," she said.

The girl glanced at Erin's arm, tucked inside her jacket. "Are you hurt? Are you that woman they're searching for?"

"Yes, I broke my wrist. I don't know if they're searching up here for me. Are you going to Richford? Can you take me there?"

"No hospital in Richford."

"I know, but if you take me to the border so I can call my fiancée to come for me, I'll be okay."

"Hop on but I don't have a spare helmet."

She waved at her companion who had turned his machine around and was coming back to her.

Erin clung to the woman's back, conscious now of the pain in her arm and the fatigue in her legs. The machines roared into the town. Behind her, the sun lit the dark trees at the summit of Jay Peak. The snow machines pulled to stop at the border crossing, their riders waved to Erin, and they headed for the Canadian border.

Erin limped into the office and collapsed into a chair near the door.

"Miss?"

"I need your help."

The man at the desk raked her with suspicious eyes. He walked out and loomed over her. A hard man, she thought. Cold grey eyes and a stubborn jaw. What must she look like to him? Clothes that belonged to a bigger person, broken down boots, unwashed hair, filthy face. Perhaps he thought she was crossing the border.

"Passport."

"No, I don't have a passport. I didn't cross the border; I came off the mountain. I was kidnapped and escaped. Please check. There must be a bulletin or something about me."

"Name?"

"Erin Maxwell. I live in Culver's Mills."

He crossed to his computer and searched for a few moments and then called. Who would he call?

"Maxwell, Culver's Mills. Send me a picture."

A picture. Would she look like her photo now? Adam took the last one, on their Bermuda trip. Would he have given that one to the police? Now the man hovered, silent, waiting.

"May I call my fiancée?"

"Not yet."

"My arm's broken."

"It won't be long."

A second man came in.

"What's up?"

"Claims she was kidnapped. You hear anything about a kidnapping?"

"Yeah. When Chuck went off, he said to watch for a woman coming off the mountain."

"Didn't say that to me. A snowmobiler dropped her off."

"Did you call?"

"They're sending a picture."

Erin leaned her head back against the wall, to close her eyes for a moment.

Chapter Thirty-Two

The family waited, grouped around the fireplace. No in-laws, Anne noticed, and no children. Claire ran to them and threw her arms around her twin.

"Cecee, what happened?"

"Dad will explain. I need a soft chair and something long and alcoholic."

The twins settled on the sofa while Daniel busied himself getting drinks for all of them. They had the air of a family conference, Anne thought.

"Dad?" Claire said.

"A woman attempted to push Cecee off the road at the big hill."

The girls clutched each other's hand, but Daniel was on his feet again.

"What? Why?"

"Likely she thought Anne was the driver," Thomas said.

"But why?" Claire said.

"Who wants to kill you?" asked Cecilia

"Who wants to kill a paediatrician?" said Daniel.

Cecilia leaned forward towards her father in the opposite chair. "How did she find me?"

"I suspect when they go over the car, they'll find a bug."

Daniel paced the carpet, pausing in front of Anne but spoke to Thomas.

"A bug. What the hell, Dad? What's going on? Who is Anne?"

"You should ask who I am."

Three faces, shocked into silence, stared at their father and then turned to Anne.

"What is this?" Daniel said.

"The woman's name is Colette. In Europe, when I arrived in Setenil, a little town in Spain, she was running two agents who had kidnapped an Israeli child and were holding her there, in plain view. I grew suspicious and then a man, a man who saved my life in Bermuda, asked for a favour. He wanted to take the child back, and he wanted my help. I helped him, and your dad helped me."

"But what did you mean when you said we should ask who you are?" Cecilia said to her father.

"Are we all in danger?" Claire said, jumping to the heart of the matter, worried about her children.

"Until we stop her."

"Who are we."

"The International criminal justice system, Interpol, FBI, CIA. The woman was an agent of an arms cartel but now—"

"I think she's an agent of the Russians or a Russian who wants the jewels back," Anne said.

Daniel paused again.

"Jewels? What jewels?"

"The ones Colette stole from Erin."

"Erin Maxwell?"

"Yes. Erin's been kidnapped but escaped, and now she's lost on the mountain."

"Stop. Just stop. This is some sort of bad movie that we've come in on an hour after it started," Cecilia said.

"All of you have to know that none of this is Anne's fault. She was on vacation in Bermuda when I arrived to go to a conference. She helped destroy a plot to kill the Secretary of State and made an enemy of this woman Colette. Later, in Spain, Anne rescued a kidnapped child, and another of Colette's plans went bust. Now, here, somehow, she is searching for the Russian treasure and sees Anne in her way again."

"But why is this your fault? I'm asking, Dad, who are you?"

"I worked for the CIA, as an operative, years ago but lately as an asset at times, and now, not at all. Before you ask, I can't tell you anything about those years."

"He took an oath," Anne said. "He keeps it."

The twins huddled on the sofa, glancing at each other and at the man they thought they knew. Daniel asked the questions.

"You worked to keep the country safe?"

"Yes."

"And you had to keep us in the dark?"

"Yes."

"And Anne, is she CIA, too?"

"No," said Anne. "I'm a Canadian paediatrician with a knack for being in the wrong place at the right time."

"We'll need some time, Dad," Claire said, glanced again at Cecilia.

"Anne will be coming to stay here until I take her back to Canada," Thomas said.

News to her, Anne thought.

"But—" she said.

"We'll discuss it on the way to Culver's."

∾

Adam pushed his coffee cup, refilled too many times, across the table and leaned forward to peer through the snow toward the roar coming from the bridge. Snowmobiles, he thought, heading for the border. The last rider had a woman on behind, no helmet and brown hair blowing back from her oval face. Erin. Was that Erin? He ran out of the cafe and followed behind. How far had it been? A mile and a half, Pete said. It would take him a half hour, maybe less. She wouldn't cross the border. She'd go to the agents, ask for help, call him and they would be together again. If that was Erin.

The wind coming from the north made it seem more like three hours as he fought his way through the snow along the two-lane highway, past a golf course and some homes with Christmas trees in the windows and multi-coloured lights outlining their windows. Ahead he caught the faint glimmer of light in the back room of the border station. When he reached the door, he knocked but opened it without waiting. A small woman, enveloped in a too-big parka and winter coveralls, one arm supporting the other, her head against the wall, stirred but didn't move, didn't open her eyes.

"Hey," said the man behind the counter.

"My fiancée—"

Adam dropped to his knees beside Erin and shook her gently. She brushed away his hand.

"Why—" Her eyes opened.

"Erin, it's me, baby. It's me."

She sobbed then, clutching him like a lost child. He held her until she quieted, and sat in the chair beside her.

"Are you all right. Did he hurt you?"

"Some. He hit me and knocked out a tooth. I have it still." She pulled the little package from the filthy pocket of her stolen parka. "You take it."

"What's wrong with your arm? Did he break it?"

"No. I fell down a hill."

"He didn't...hurt you in any other way?"

"No, but he threatened that when he came back, if you hadn't given him the egg, he would make me pay. What egg? Did he think I had an Imperial Russian Egg? What will he do now? He'll—"

"No, he's dead. His handler killed him. You're safe now. You're safe."

"Do you folks want to call someone?" the border agent asked.

"Did you get the information about me that you needed?" said Erin.

"Yes, ma'am. Would you like a coffee now?"

"Do you have anything to eat?"

Adam called the rescue team and told them Erin was safe and arranged for someone to pick them up. Erin drank coffee and ate someone's lunch and told Adam what had happened with Ivan.

"What about his handler?" asked the border agent.

A cold hand gripped Erin's chest.

"Is she still out there? What will she do?"

"They'll find her."

Ten minutes later, they were in the back of a cruiser, on their way to Culver's Mills.

Quin clicked off his phone. In a few hours, Colette could be over the border, but would she go without the jewels, her clothes? He thought she would. If she couldn't get the egg, she would need to disappear. If Alexei were in charge, she would be in deep trouble. What had she done when the op went south in Spain? Cleaned house and disappeared. She wasn't a field agent. She was used to being a conduit, a go-between but she also wasn't used to failure. She had a good run until Anne stopped the success.

And the fiasco in Spain. She would blame Anne for that too. She likely thought Anne was an agent, not an innocent bystander. Would she want revenge? If it came down to the egg or revenge, he bet she would choose the egg, but...

He cleaned up his motel room, packed the few clothes he had, and checked out.

An hour later he reached the outskirts of Culver's Mills and Catherine's road. He drove by, noted Thomas's SUV parked in front and turned the corner. A helmeted person on a motorcycle, head down, texting. He passed and a few blocks later, drove back. No motorcycle. He pulled in behind the SUV and opened his passenger window a crack, enough for sound, anyway. Snow blew in across his face, drifting against the windows, dying there in tiny puddles. It blanketed the town, shrouding the trees, slowing the traffic out on the freeway, so the engines purred past. From where he sat, he couldn't see the yard at the back of the house. But he heard a motor-cycle, something big, like the Harley he passed earlier. Was the rider texting and to whom or was that a bit of show, to reassure him that the rider wasn't watching the house?

He climbed out of the car and crept onto the porch. He listened at the door, heard nothing, and tapped.

Anne and Thomas and maybe the motorcycle rider were in there, but no one answered. He hesitated, not wanting to burst in on some private affair, but worked the locks with his picks. A moment later and he was inside. Still quiet. What were they doing?

Chapter Thirty-Three

Anne grasped the bar above the passenger door of the SUV, climbed on the running board and swung into her seat.

"I think I'm must be getting shorter," she said.

"No, more tired," he said.

He stroked her arm once before he grasped the wheel and put the big vehicle in gear.

"What's this about me staying out here?" she said. "Cecilia doesn't want me."

"With what we told them, they may want neither of us."

He looked at her profile, her jaw rigid with emotion, her eyes straight ahead.

"Anne?"

"How can we have a future if Colette is hunting me or us, if Cecilia decides that she won't accept me? I thought we were making progress but now—"

"I made it clear I involved you, and if she or they didn't hear that, I'll repeat it until they do. My future must include you. It must."

She was silent. What was she thinking? Was it over between them? How could it be over? So much had happened. They shared so much.

But if he was honest with himself, what they shared was danger —here, where their plane crashed, and they walked together to safety, in Bermuda, in Spain, and now here, again. They hadn't had much time for banal, day to day, get up in the morning and have coffee, time with each other.

"Anne?" he said.

A quick glance told him she was stiff, her eyes focussed somewhere outside the car.

"All the parts of a family don't get along all the time, but when one of the family thinks the other is...what? An interloper, someone who is a thief who is going to steal her father away from her—"

"It's not you now, but my past life that is troubling her and the rest. Claire is worried about her children, and so is Daniel. With Cecilia, it's more about the lies."

"Necessary lies."

"I'm not sure she sees it that way."

"I'm going home, Thomas. I'll come back if you want my help with your mother, but I need time at home, in my own space, in my own country."

Ahead, the old clapboard house appeared through the snow.

"We can talk about it later. For now, let's collect your stuff and go back to the house."

"You think we'll be safe from her there?"

"Yes. Quin will get her or at least scare her off."

He parked in front of the B&B. Drifts clogged the sidewalk to the house, and Thomas ploughed ahead to make a path for Anne. At the door, she fumbled with the key. He resisted the urge to take it from her. He would always have to resist the urge to help her. At last, the door opened, Anne switched on the light and took off her boots and coat.

He put his arms around her for a moment.

"Do you want to stay here for a while, to be alone together?"

"For a little while. Would you like a drink? There's scotch on the sideboard in the dining room."

"What would you like?"

"Cinzano, I think."

He poured the drinks, carried them into the library and sat beside her on the worn green couch.

"To us," he said.

"To us."

Outside a motorcycle roared down the street and a few moments later he heard it in the lane behind the house.

"I'm going to check," he said. "That sound came from the back."

After their visits to the hospital and the dentist, Adam and Erin climbed the stairs to their apartment. Adam set the alarm to *stay at home* and hung his jacket up on a brass hook beside Erin's. From the kitchen, he heard the sound of water splashing into the kettle. Tea, Erin's answer to stress. He needed a whiskey. He poured it and helped Erin with the tray of cups and teapot.

Later, they huddled together on the sofa, the only light the twinkling from the Christmas tree set in front of the window.

"I thought I lost you," he said.

She snuggled deeper into his arms.

"I knew you'd find me."

He reached into his pocket for the letter he'd been carrying since Erin went missing. Should he tell her now? They had to decide together but was now the right time? She stirred and sat up.

"What is it?"

How did she always know?

"I got a letter today in answer to the FBI application."

"And?"

"Yes."

Her brown eyes, shining with tears, turned to meet his.

"How wonderful. That's what you've wanted."

"Is it what you want?"

"Of course, it is. How can you ask?"

"The shop?"

Adam walked to the kitchen and came back with a plateful of cheese and crackers.

"The shop?" he said again.

Erin reached for a cracker and loaded on some still-cold Brie.

"Is a shop. I can put the stock in storage, give the owner notice, and we're free to leave. How long will you be in Washington?"

"Twenty weeks. That's a long time to be apart, Erin."

Erin leaned back and closed her eyes. Her eyelids looked bruised over her pale cheeks. Why hadn't he kept it to himself? Too much for her to deal with after what she had gone through.

"You have to live there? On site."

"Yes."

"What about weekends?"

"I'll have to ask. Would you want to move to Washington for twenty weeks?"

"Perhaps not. I could use the time to wind up the shop, have sales, that sort of thing."

He put his arms around her.

"We don't have to decide now, not now."

"When?"

"They want an answer by the fifth."

"Of January?"

"Yes. Can you decide by then?"

"No deciding needed. It's too good an opportunity to miss, and it's what you've wanted."

"What about your plans?"

"My plans are to be with you."

At that, he tucked her head under his chin. Tears threatened, and he raised one hand to knuckle them away.

∼

Colette tapped her fingers. What took her so long? The nun promised to fetch the Mother Superior of the convent.

The calm voice of the Mother Superior, her teacher when she was a child, came through the phone.

"So, is all well?"

"Not yet. I hope I can be with you in three or four days. I have a little business to transact, and then I shall drive to the nearest international airport. How is she?"

"Confused. Missing her friends and wondering if she is being punished for something. She is becoming very sad."

Colette held the phone against her forehead for a moment.

"Tell her I will be there very soon and all will be as it was."

Moments later, she placed a call to Alexei.

"I have it."

"The egg?"

"Yes. Where can we meet?"

"There is a small town called Greenbank, a short distance from Culver's Mills. I will meet you there in one hour."

"Where?"

"There is a gas station on the east side. There."

"Fine."

Half-an-hour later, she sat in the rental car, waiting for Alexei to arrive. When he did, she left her car before he could get out of his. She carried a package in her left hand. His face appeared in the side mirror of the car, watching. She kept her right arm swinging far from her body until she walked into the blind spot in the car's mirror. Alexei lowered the window. She placed the muzzle of the silencer against his neck.

"You should not have threatened my daughter, Alexei."

"I wouldn't have—"

But he couldn't tell her what he wouldn't have done, and now he never would. She slapped the top of the car and walked away.

She drove back into Culver's Mills. On a side street in the industrial area, she left the keys in the car and strode off. Thirty minutes later, she stole a motorcycle from a dealership. The memory of riding her own Harley through the Swiss mountains came back to her as she negotiated the slush-covered streets. She eased into a parking spot with a clear view of the front door of the B&B and waited.

An hour later, cold seeped into her bones, but still, she waited. Her reward came soon. McPhail climbed out of an SUV and walked up the steps of the house. So small to make so much trouble, Colette thought. Behind her, a man locked the vehicle and followed her into the house. The lights turned on in the front room, the one with the safe. She put the bike in gear and circled the block to the lane behind the B&B. She switched it off and raced down the path to the kitchen door. She hid out of sight of the windows and doors and waited. If they heard the motorcycle, one of them would come. Him, she hoped. She wanted to deal with the woman at leisure.

She heard old floorboards creaking, and the door opened. She raised her arm and struck.

Chapter Thirty-Four

When Thomas left to check the back, Anne ran to the safe. Her fingers, wet with fear, slipped on the numbers. She wiped her hands on her shirt and began again. The door lock clicked, she grabbed the case, and hid behind the sofa. She inserted the magazine in the gun and waited. Was that a voice? Was Thomas calling her? No, just the wind in the chimney, whispering. Her heart raced, and her breaths came in ragged bursts. Stop. She willed her breathing to slow.

"McPhail? I'm coming for you. Your friend won't rescue you."

Thomas. What did she do to Thomas?

"Why are you doing this?"

"You ruined my life, and now I'm a killer."

"You never killed before you came here?"

"No. And that Russian attacked me. I wouldn't have eyes if I'd let her reach me."

"Self-defence, then?"

Colette didn't sound any closer but waiting at the door. She expected that Anne would be armed.

"Yes. And Ivan. He wanted to kill me."

"He had a gun."

"Yes, but that doesn't matter. Even if I escape from here, from the Americans, the Russians will still be after me, and Interpol."

Her voice sounded closer. She was in the room now.

"I'm coming for you and then we will go somewhere, and you will die slowly."

Anne laughed. She couldn't help it. The melodrama.

"Come on, Colette. Torture. You? You spent your time behind a desk, tapping on a computer with long red nails."

"What does it matter, whether they are red or purple or gold?"

"It says who you are. Clean hands."

"Not now."

"But again. If you left now. If you ran for the border. You must have documents, somewhere. Cross the border. Go to Montreal, disappear. Get on a plane and return to Switzerland. Don't you have another identity there?"

"Leave you alive and slink back to Europe with the shards of my life?"

Anne edged around the sofa, hidden by the high arm. Where was she? At the safe?

"You have a weapon," Colette said.

"Yes."

"You won't shoot. That was your profile. Non-violent. Hates guns."

"Who do you think shot Esti?"

"You, you killed her? I don't believe you."

"She attacked me. The gun went off."

"This is different. You would fire at a target, a human target. Do you know how?"

"The Mossad agent taught me."

But she wouldn't be able to. In Spain, she defended Naomi, an innocent child, but shoot Colette, take a life to save her own. No.

Silence. Was she moving? In the distance, she heard the wail of the sirens.

"You haven't done anything except defend yourself here. Go, Colette. Escape. You can do it. It's only an hour to the border. I don't want to shoot you. I'm not an agent. I can't arrest you, and I don't want to die. Do you hear the sirens? They're coming."

"I'll take you as a hostage."

"What for? You want to escape, not make a deal. Go."

More silence and then the sound of feet running down the hall and the kitchen door's familiar slam. A few moments later, the roar of the motorcycle. Thomas. What had she done to Thomas?

At the back door, she found him, crumpled on the step, blood staining the snow around his head. She felt for his pulse.

Quin stood in the hallway, his weapon in his hand. Sirens. Someone saw Colette or him. He checked the library and the living room across the hall and crept to the kitchen. Cold air blasted into the warm room, filling it with swirls of snow. A figure in the doorway, a silhouette against the light, bent double.

"I have a weapon trained on you," he said.

"Quin? Quin, it's Anne. Help me. She hit Thomas. He's unconscious. There's so much blood."

She wavered, but Quin was there, holding her.

"If he's bleeding, he's alive. Call 911. I'll get him inside."

He lifted Thomas who moaned and tried to walk before he slumped into Quin's arms.

"They're coming," Anne said.

Quin laid Thomas on the floor. Anne knelt beside him, cradling his head in kitchen towels, whispering.

"Where did she go?"

Confused for a moment, she shook her head and then she remembered. Colette. How did Quin know?

"Away. She said she killed Dasha and Ivan in self-defence. I told her she could still escape. She hit Thomas; she didn't kill him. She could have, but she didn't. She didn't."

"You don't think she's a killer."

"I think she's pragmatic. Where would you go?"

"The border. I'll look for Colette in Montreal."

"You won't alert the border?"

"No. I want her. She knows things."

"Then go. I'll be here when the ambulance comes. I'll tell Pete."

He hesitated, his hand on Anne's arm. Stalwart, he thought. That's what she was. Stalwart.

"Until next time."

The ambulance pulled into the back lane, and the paramedics raced across the backyard.

"You told them the back."

"Yes. You can leave by the front."

He walked away, back through the house, down the steps and across to his rental. An hour later he crossed the border at Richford.

Chapter Thirty-Five

Anne perched on a kitchen chair, its wooden back pressing into hers. The paramedics scolded her for moving him.

"He was half in, half out. I had to."

Pete came and took her statement and checked the safe and her gun.

"You didn't fire?"

"No. I talked to her, and she left."

"Left to go where?"

"I don't know; I don't know."

Her breath caught in a sob and she put her head in her hands.

"I'll talk to you later," he said, aiming a clumsy pat at her shoulder that glanced off her head.

The routine of the assessment carried on in silence broken only by murmurs from the paramedics—his vital signs, his temperature, his cardiac status—and then the collar for his neck and the intravenous lines, two of them, and then they lifted him onto the stretcher and took him.

"I want to ride with him."

"Ma'am, there's no room—"

"I'm a doctor. I've ridden many times, and I know there's room. I won't be any trouble to you."

They let her, rather than argue any longer. The ride was brief, a few minutes to the cottage hospital his family endowed.

In the ER, the process in reverse—moving him to the stretcher in the trauma room and then a nurse urged her away from his bedside so they could work.

Thomas, his mobile face still, his skin pale, roused enough to knock the doctor's hand away when she assessed his response to pain.

"He walked a little, from where we found him, to the kitchen," she said to the air.

The doctor grunted. Had she heard her?

They wheeled him away for a CAT scan, and she walked back to the waiting room and slumped in a chair. The dark orange fabric, worn and tired from holding too many grieving relatives, was rough under her hands. The children, she thought. She should call the children.

"Daniel, it's Anne. Thomas is injured, and I'm in the ER, waiting. Can you come?"

"What hospital?"

"Here, in Culver's."

"I'll be right there."

A few minutes later, Daniel and the twins raced through the waiting room door.

"Where is he," said Cecilia.

"CAT scan."

"What happened?"

"The woman who stalked us, the woman who tried to push you off the road, hit him, likely with the butt of her gun. She wanted to kill me, but I talked and talked. She left. She just left, and I found Thomas, at the back door."

"Why?"

"We'll tell you later when Thomas is home."

The doors to the ER opened, and the doctor strode over to them.

"Are you Thomas's family?"

"Yes," said Daniel.

"His CAT scan was okay, and he's awake now. Which of you is Anne?"

"I am."

"He's asking for you."

Anne turned to the others.

"I'll stay a minute and come back."

"But—"

"No, Cecee. He asked for Anne," her twin said, holding her sister's hand.

"I'll be right back."

She stood at Thomas's bedside. For a moment, she didn't speak. What he had done for the CIA; who he had been: none of it mattered. She loved him."

"Annie."

"I'm here."

He opened his eyes and moved his hand towards her. She held it and bent over to kiss him.

"How?"

"You're going to be okay. No fractures, no bleeding."

"Us."

"We're okay too. The children are here, and they should see you."

She went to the waiting room door and beckoned. Daniel and Cecilia came.

"Two at a time," she said, walked over to the row of chairs and sat beside Claire.

The young woman turned laid her head on Anne's shoulder and clutched her hand.

"He'll be all right, Claire. He'll be fine."

Anne met Erin and Adam at the front door of the Beauchamp home. Erin, her face glowing from the cold, jaunty in a scarlet tuque and mittens, hugged Anne.

"Thank you for all you did to find me."

"I did very little. It was Adam and his determination to find you."

"Mrs. Beauchamp?" Adam asked. He too was bundled against the cold, in a down-filled, khaki parka.

"Still alive but gravely ill. You never know who will survive. Some people are so resilient."

In the foyer, they handed their coats to the maid and slipped off their boots. Anne carried a blue bag, woven with images of snowflakes that she kept with her. Another family meeting in the conservatory. She took Thomas's hand. How pale and wan, he looked, she thought.

"How are you?"

"Good. A bit of a headache, but that should pass. The girls are giving good imitations of mother hens."

"Dad," the twins said.

"I promised we would tell them what was going on."

"Starting with Bermuda? That's a long tale."

"No, starting with Erin."

Erin, sitting opposite in a leather club chair, her charming smile no longer marred by a missing tooth, sat up and held her hands together in her lap.

"I received a commission from a law firm to evaluate some jewellery and objets d'art. The jewellery was Russian and had a Fabergé hallmark. I satisfied myself, and two consultants agreed, that they were genuine. The objects were another story. Two hideous statues, one of a loaf of bread and the other of a fish, without signatures or provenance of any kind, were of little value, or so I thought until the woman was murdered in my shop."

"That's where I came in," Anne said. "I interrupted a scene between Erin and a Russian couple who were demanding that Erin return the jewellery, claiming the pieces belonged to them. The next day, I found the woman dead at the back of the shop. Later that day, Ivan, one of the Russians, kidnapped Erin."

Adam reached for Erin's hand.

"That's when he demanded the egg and kept on demanding it until he returned to the B&B and Colette shot him," Anne said.

"Colette?"

"A woman Thomas and I crossed paths with, in Bermuda and Spain. A Russian handler sent her to recover the egg, and she employed Ivan and Dasha, but they failed. She hates me because she blames me for upsetting all her plans. But when she could have stayed and killed me, she didn't."

"Why, or rather why not?" asked Adam.

"I don't know but I talked and talked, trying to convince her that she wasn't a murderer yet, that she had shot in self-defence and then she heard the sirens and ran out."

There was more, more about Thomas, more about Quin, but no one asked the right questions, and she didn't volunteer.

"All the time, you were lost in the woods?" Claire asked Erin.

"Not lost. Not entirely lost. I knew about where I was and what direction to walk in, and where I thought I could get help. Some strangers on snow machines helped me and then Adam came."

"But what about the egg?" Cecilia asked.

Anne said. "I must tell you that I went to see Mrs. Akers today. She invited me to visit her because she had kept back a piece of information. The family story was a bit more complicated than a grateful Empress giving such a valuable gift to a maid. It was always an unbelievable story, but now it makes perhaps a little more sense. She told me that this egg was one the Empress hated. The outside was red enamel, and the red reminded her of blood and her grandson's torment from his hemophilia. She gave it to Mrs. Akers' ancestor to destroy, but she didn't. Whether the story is true or whether this is one of the eggs that Fabergé made for other clients is for experts to decide. I think the jewellery alone is enough to ensure Mrs. Akers can stay in her retirement home or another, equally comfortable palliative care home."

"So where is the egg?" Cecilia said.

"I got a clue from the paintings in your hallway. This is old news to Claire, but the fish plays an important part in ancient Christian iconography. Early Christians used the symbol as a way to identify each other. I think that's why we have the loaf and a fish."

"Both hideous," said Claire.

"Yes, But I think this one has a secret. Mrs. Akers gave me permission to search for it."

Anne took a tea towel from her bag and spread it on the floor. She tapped the fish with a small hammer and the outer layer shattered, revealing within a red-enamelled egg, encrusted with jewels.

"There should be a surprise," Anne said, undoing the clasp.

An exquisite basket of flowers, modelled in yellows and pinks, lay nestled within the egg.

"How lovely," said Erin. "but is it one of the missing Easter eggs?"

"Perhaps not, but Fabergé made them for others, and some of those have never been found. Or it may be genuine. There are two years with no known orders for Easter gifts. This may be from one of those years."

The maid appeared with coffee, and they sat in silence, looking at the three inches of gilt and enamel and jewels that had caused so much misery.

"We'll return everything to the lawyers. They can handle it for Mrs. Akers," said Adam.

"We have news," Erin said. "Adam is going to the FBI at Quantico, and when he is posted, unless it's Burlington, we'll be moving."

"Oh, Erin. Your lovely shop," said Anne.

"I wouldn't be able to keep it when the baby comes."

And that was the best news of all.

Chapter Thirty-Six

The yellow plane idled on the runway, waiting to fly them back to Canada.

"Will you stay for a time or will you fly right back?" Daniel asked his father.

They stood at the door, Thomas dressed again in his camel-hair overcoat, his head still bandaged from Colette's attack.

"I'll be staying in Toronto for a day for a business meeting, and I'll drive Anne to Bridgenorth. I'll be back by New Year's Eve."

"Are you coming back for the New Year?" Daniel asked Anne.

"No," said Anne. "Your family needs some time."

Daniel reached out and drew her into a hug.

"We don't, none of us, feel that way, Anne."

Anne patted his back and said, "Thank you for that, but I need to be at home for a while."

A few moments later they climbed into the back seat. His head injury still sidelined Thomas from flying. The ground fell away, became a map again as they flew north to Buttonville, near Toronto. He reached for Anne's hand.

"Are we okay?"

"It's hard to believe, but we are more okay than I think we ever have been."

"Yes?"

"When I watched them work in the ER, I knew that I loved you and I had to make this, our relationship work."

"I love you, too. We'll make it work, even if it's long distance for most of the time."

He kissed her and tucked her hand into his. She leaned against his shoulder and slept. When she awoke, it was to see the city spread below them. So many trees, she thought, pleased the city was building up the urban forest. The creeks and rivers gleamed in the sunshine, running in heavily forested ravines towards Lake Ontario.

When they landed at the small airport north of Toronto, a car driven by one of Thomas's employees picked them up.

"Thanks for coming out in the holiday," Thomas said to him.

"You're welcome, sir."

Three-quarters of an hour later, they stood looking at the lake from the window in Anne's condo, a five-hundred square foot pied-à-terre. Prosecco sparkled in the glasses they both held.

"Would you like to come with me on a business trip next month?"

"Somewhere south?"

He laughed and said, "No, Haliburton. We'd fly into an island a client owns."

"Why not? A lovely winter holiday."

She clinked glasses with Thomas and sipped her wine.

Chapter Thirty-Seven

I n Switzerland, Quin cleared customs and shook hands with the man who waited for him.

"Winston. Good to see you. Do you know where she is?"

"No, but I know where she will come. She has a daughter."

About the Author

Virginia Winters is a retired paediatrician who lives in Kawartha Lakes, Ontario, Canada. *The Jewelled Egg Murders* is the fifth book in her series, *Dangerous Journeys*.

To reach Virginia:

www.virginiawinters.ca
vwinters@bell.net